For more than forty years,
Yearling has been the leading name
in classic and award-winning literature
for young readers.

Yearling books feature children's
favorite authors and characters,
providing dynamic stories of adventure,
humor, history, mystery, and fantasy.

Trust Yearling paperbacks to entertain,
inspire, and promote the love of reading
in all children.

**OTHER YEARLING BOOKS
YOU WILL ENJOY**

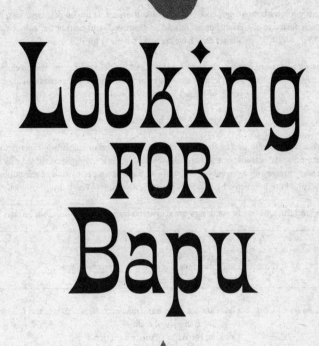

Looking
FOR
Bapu

◆

ANJALI BANERJEE

A YEARLING BOOK

Published by Yearling
an imprint of Random House Children's Books
a division of Random House, Inc., New York

This is a work of fiction. Names, characters, places, and incidents either are the product of the author's imagination or are used fictitiously. Any resemblance to actual persons, living or dead, events, or locales is entirely coincidental.

Visit us on the Web! www.randomhouse.com/kids

Educators and librarians, for a variety of teaching tools,
visit us at www.randomhouse.com/teachers

The Library of Congress has cataloged the hardcover edition of this work as follows:
Banerjee, Anjali.
Looking for Bapu / Anjali Banerjee.
p. cm.
Summary: When his beloved grandfather dies, eight-year-old Anu feels that his spirit is near and will stop at nothing to bring him back, including trying to become a Hindu holy man.
ISBN: 978-0-385-74657-1 (trade) — ISBN: 978-0-385-90894-8 (lib. bdg.)
[1. Grandfathers—Fiction. 2. Death—Fiction. 3. Hindus—Fiction. 4. East Indian Americans—Fiction. 5. Schools—Fiction. 6. Northwest, Pacific—Fiction.]
I. Title.
[Fic]—dc22
2006002021

ISBN: 978-0-553-49425-9 (pbk.)
Reprinted by arrangement with Wendy Lamb Books
Printed in the United States of America
August 2008
10 9 8 7 6 5 4 3 2
First Yearling Edition

In memory of my grandfathers,

Siddhartha Banerjee and Atul Chandra Roy

and my dear friend Dotty Sohl

Your searching mind at last

finds the object of the search within

your own heart.

—Yajur Veda 32.11

CHAPTER 1

Garuda, the Hindu god of birds, is also the king of bird poop. When he brings finches and nuthatches to our feeders, the droppings fertilize the soil. So he's also the god of new grass. He flies direct from India to Seattle, and it doesn't matter that the airports have been closed for a week since the planes hit the Twin Towers.

Garuda has the wings of an eagle.

My grandfather Bapu prays to all the gods and goddesses, but he's silent as we trek into the woods to search for barred owls. Bapu marches ahead and I copy his strides, stepping into his giant bootprints in the soil. I'm Anu the Boy Explorer, star of *National Geographic*, bringing my backpack and birdseed to feed the chickadees.

"Quiet, Shona," Bapu whispers. He still uses my Bengali

baby nickname, which means "golden," although I'm already eight and three-quarters.

I try to be quiet, but my jeans swish and my breathing disturbs the leaves. The air smells of fall—of dampness and leaves. Afternoon sunlight filters through the treetops, and a breeze lifts my hair. No biplanes or helicopters buzz overhead. The sky sleeps in a strange silence.

Bapu makes many turns, tramples far off the path and finally stops in a clearing. We're far from the house; I can't see the moss-covered roof.

I sit next to Bapu, so close that his warmth radiates into my leg. His clove and sweet pipe smell mixes with the cotton laundry scent of his shirt.

My heart beats fast.

"Soon, Anu, soon," he says.

I check every shadow, watch for an owl blending in against a tree trunk. The barred owl hunts by night but also by day, Bapu says. He knows everything. He can name birds by their calls, and he knew it would rain today. The sky clouds over and drizzle spits down. We wait and watch until my legs cramp and then we pull on our ponchos and we're two yellow mushrooms sprouting from the ground. The drizzle turns to rain, and Bapu takes a folded umbrella from his pocket, pops it open above our heads. His fingers quiver.

If my best friend, Unger, were here, he would complain about the rain streaking up his glasses. The only birds he watches are the plastic ones you use to play badminton.

"How long do we wait?" I whisper, tapping my foot. I pick up a pebble, drop it, pick it up, drop it.

2

Bapu presses a finger to his lips and nods his head in the Indian style, halfway between *no* and *yes*. "Patience, Shona. Like the sadhus of India, nah? They meditate for many years in caves without complaint."

I tap my fingers in the damp moss. "Don't they get bored?"

"They leave all thoughts and feelings behind. They strive for that which is unknowable to the human mind."

"If it's unknowable, why do they waste their time striving?"

"Striving is the whole point. They pursue their own inner light." He points to my chest. "You have inner light."

I have my own built-in lightbulb? Like the dome light that goes on when you open the car door? All I can feel is my heartbeat. "Do the birds have inner light too?"

Bapu waves an arm in a sweeping motion. "The light is everywhere, part of the Absolute, shimmering in everything."

His words swirl out and sparkle like magic dust. I try to imagine the inner lightbulbs glowing in the raindrops, in the leaves, in the dirt beneath my fingernails. "I can't see the special light, Bapu. Is there a switch?"

He chuckles and pats my head. "Ah, Shona. You'll see. Perhaps you'll have to meditate for a full twelve years as the holy men do!"

"Twelve years?" I'm not even nine. "I could never wait that long."

"When your heart aches, you're willing to wait." Bapu presses a hand to his chest. "I waited two years for your Amma, until her father gave his permission for the marriage—"

"A whole two years?" I picture Bapu meditating day after day, not even getting up to eat or pee while he waits for Amma. I never got to meet her. She died before I was born.

"Two years is but a moment in the large scheme of time, Shona."

"I'm just over four moments old, then. Two times four equals eight."

"Your life is a god's hiccup, but an important hiccup."

I imagine the bird-god, Garuda, hiccupping me up, and I glance at the sky, in case he swoops down to swallow me.

"*Bhalo*, enough for today, Shona, nah?"

We get up and hike back through the woods. No owl today. We made too much noise, but I like talking to Bapu. He holds all the knowledge of the universe in his enormous, ancient brain.

He's walking so slowly that I bump into him, and then he stumbles and falls on his face. The umbrella goes flying and lands with a thump. He must have tripped over a root. I wait for him to get up.

"Bapu, you okay? Let's go."

He doesn't reply.

"Bapu?"

I kneel beside him.

"Bapu?" His fingers aren't trembling anymore, but he's breathing. His lips are turning blue the way my lips get when I'm cold. Bapu's cold, way too cold. Why won't he talk to me? Why won't he move? My stomach does a somersault. Something terrible is happening.

I drop my pack and run.

4

CHAPTER 2

The branches grow thicker and brambles snag my jeans. Which way? Where is the path? I should have remembered where Bapu stepped. His bootprints are gone. Where is our roof? Nothing but tall trees blocking the light. I'm going the wrong way.

My breath comes in short gasps. This way, no, that way. What do I do? How do I remember where I've been? A chickadee scolds me, and I remember the birdseed in my pocket. I drop a trail of seed as I run. The rain stops, and sunlight slants sideways through the trees.

Why didn't I bring the cell phone? I left it on the kitchen counter next to the cordless. I'm so stupid. I should have put it in my pocket, no matter what Bapu said about being quiet in the woods. I'm running forever, and then I see a glimmer of our roof, steam rising from the moss.

I'm inside and my fingers shake as I punch 911 on the phone. I'm babbling, birdseed spilling onto the floor.

A nice lady with a calm voice tells me to stay on the line while she sends an ambulance. She's asking my name and I accidentally say Siddhartha Ganguli, Bapu's real name, because I can't think straight.

"Is your mother home, Siddhartha?" she asks.

"I'm not Siddhartha, I'm Anu. My parents aren't home yet, just me."

"Stay there so you can show the medics where your grandfather is." She asks how far Bapu is from the house, where in the woods. Down the path, around the bend, and I have to go back to him before all the chickadees eat the seed; his nose must be full of dirt. Maybe the dirt is sliding down his throat into his lungs. Hurry, hurry, I say, and my teeth chatter and the house feels cold although the heat is on.

"What's your address, honey?"

"Six nine four Orca Lane. In Oyster Cove."

"How old is your grandfather?"

"Seventy-three."

"Is he on any medications?"

"I don't know—his fingers shake."

I answer a million silly questions and then a siren screams up our driveway. I hang up and run out to the ambulance, its red lights whirring. Two men and a blond lady with muscles climb out. They grab bags and a stretcher and we're running through the woods again. Running forever. They're asking me which way.

6

"Follow the seed."

"Smart kid," the tall medic says.

"A little Islam, ain't he?" the short one mumbles. He's the driver. He doesn't think I heard him.

"Come on, Dave," the tall one says.

My throat tightens. I want to yell that the word is *Muslim*, not *Islam*, and I'm not a Muslim anyway, but I don't have time to explain.

"He's here." I'm gasping, kneeling beside Bapu, who is wet and covered with dirt. When did that happen? He looks crumpled. "Bapu! Bapu. I'm here."

"Hang in there, little man." The tall medic pulls me out of the way while the others kneel beside Bapu.

"Like that damned bin Laden," the short man mutters. "Check out the beard."

"Stop it, Dave!" the blond woman says.

What has this got to do with Bapu? "You have to help him. He got cold and he tripped."

His face looks calm, as if he's secretly talking to the gods. I pick up the wet umbrella.

The medics are poking a needle in his arm and taking his pulse and talking into a headpiece, reciting numbers and words. I'm getting colder and my legs are logs, but I have to stay with Bapu. He needs me.

"The kid's in shock." The woman glances at me.

"Let's get a blanket to warm you up," the tall medic says. He puts a hand on my shoulder, but I shrug him off. They're strapping Bapu onto a stretcher.

"I have to go with him." I run after them.

"Whoa—take it easy, little man," the tall medic says.

They bounce Bapu all the long way back through the woods—they have to find a clear path for the stretcher. His face is grayish, but it must be the fading light. He looks just like my Bapu—same beard, long nose, shiny bald head—but his eyes won't open and he doesn't hear me.

They let me climb into the ambulance with him because there's no time and no adult here to care for me. Don't they understand? I care for Bapu, and Bapu cares for me. Sometimes I wish, and I hate that I wish this, that it was just Bapu and me. I love Ma and Dad, but they work all the time. And they make rules. Bapu lets me stay up late when they're not home. He cooks my favorite Indian food and reads Indian comics to me before bed. He tells secrets about the Hindu gods and holy men.

I'm riding in the back of the ambulance with the tall medic and the blond lady, who lets me hold Bapu's hand. His fingers feel cold.

"Bapu—wake up." I glance at the blond lady. "Will he be okay?"

"We're doing all we can, honey. You keep talking to him."

The swerving ambulance makes me want to hurl. "Bapu, it's time for your glass of whisky. I have to beat you at checkers. You said you would make *payesh* tonight." *Payesh* is my favorite Bengali dessert, made with milk and rice and sugar. "You have to help me with homework."

He doesn't speak. His eyelashes don't even flutter.

At the hospital, the doctors whisk him away and leave me wrapped in a blanket in the waiting room. A skinny nurse brings me hot chocolate in a Styrofoam cup.

"Your parents will be here soon," she says. "Do you want to change out of that poncho and those soggy boots?"

"They're my bird-watching gear."

"Okay, then." She puts the cup on the table. "Drink the whole cup. Just read and relax and—"

"How's my Bapu? How is he?"

"We're doing everything we can for him." Her voice is feather-soft but she glances at her watch.

After she leaves, I pretend to watch the cartoons on TV. They must have given me a special waiting room. There's nobody else in here. I feel empty, cut in half. Ma always said Bapu and I were twins with the same determined jaw and walk—long strides, shoulders back—except Bapu is old and tall. He's bald with a scratchy white beard, while I have an overload of black hair, like Dad. *Like that damned bin Laden.* That's what the short man, Dave, said. At school, Curtis calls me *Osama bin Laden,* even though I could never plan an attack on a potato bug, let alone the World Trade Center. Neither could Bapu. How could anyone think my Bapu is bad? He's pure and good, and I love him so much that my teeth ache.

Ma and Dad come rushing in, Ma still in her white medical coat from her office across town, Dad in his tweed jacket from the university, his hair sticking up. Even his beard looks like it ran through a hurricane.

"Anu, baby!" Ma hugs me tightly. "Are you all right? Where's Bapu?"

"They took him—he fell in the woods. He won't wake up."

"Nurse!" Dad dashes out of the room, and in the hallway the nurse tells him he can't see Bapu because the doctors are working on him. "He's my father, damn it! I have to see him, now!" Dad rushes around, shouting questions, his voice cracking. "Is he alive?"

9

"He's alive," the nurse says. "But he's suffered a massive stroke, and I'm afraid he's slipped into a coma."

"Damn it!" Dad yells, and then his voice fades down the hall. What is a massive stroke? Something invisible and heavy. A Massive Stroke fell on Bapu, knocked him out, pressed his nose into the dirt. My fingers go numb, and my teeth still chatter. I've never heard Dad yell that loud. My dad doesn't yell at all.

Ma sits beside me and rests an arm around my shoulders. Her hand feels light compared to Bapu's. "How are you? Are you okay, baby?" She takes off her glasses. She looks bare without them, like a turtle without a shell.

"Can you save Bapu, Ma?" My voice comes out raspy. Ma's a doctor. Maybe she can fix Bapu, but she operates on stomachs and Bapu has dirt up his nose. Does Ma know about noses?

"The doctors here are excellent," she says, hugging me.

I silently ask Garuda, king of flight, to swoop down and save Bapu, to pull the Massive Stroke off him. I can't remember any other gods right now.

"Tell me what happened," Ma says, her arm around me. She glances at the TV.

I tell her as best I can.

"Whatever happened, baby, it wasn't your fault," Ma says. "Bapu would've fallen anyway, in the woods or at home, okay? This had nothing to do with you."

She's wrong. I didn't run fast enough. I let Bapu get too cold. Now my teeth are chattering, even with the blanket around me.

"Let's get you out of those clothes, okay?" Ma tries to pull off the poncho but I squirm out of her grip and sit in another chair. I can't concentrate when she squishes me.

I keep praying to Garuda. I make a bargain. I will be good.

I will do all my homework. I'll ignore Curtis calling me names. I won't imagine tripping him or punching him. I'll spend hours sitting still in the woods, not moving, not thinking, not breathing while I look for a barred owl. I count to fifty. When I get to fifty, the nurse will come and say Bapu woke up. I will practice short division and not steal sweets before supper. When Bapu arranged offerings around the statue of Lord Shiva in his room, I stole a handful of fennel. I won't do that again, ever. I don't need presents for Christmas. I could go maybe five Christmases without presents or a tree. I don't need Christmas ever again.

Is that enough? I can pray every morning. I don't chant prayers the way Bapu does. I don't understand Bengali. But I could pray, and I will, if you save Bapu.

Ma comes over to sit beside me. She holds the cup of hot chocolate to my lips and rubs my back, and I take a sip. The liquid tastes so sweet and warm, I could drown in it. Then a doctor comes in—he doesn't have Dad with him. Where is Dad? The doctor shoves his hands in the pockets of his white coat. Why do doctors always wear white? We stand up immediately. "How is he?" Ma asks.

"I'm sorry," the doctor says. "We did what we could."

"What? Oh, no." Ma collapses into the chair. It's just me standing there, staring at the doctor.

"Can I see Bapu?" I ask. I'm shaking, my knees wobbly.

"I'm sorry, son," the doctor says. "Your grandfather passed away a few minutes ago."

"No! No! My Bapu didn't die!" Someone else is screaming, a stupid little kid with my voice.

Dad comes in, his face glistening with tears, his eyes red, and he and Ma hug so tightly, they could be one person. I've never seen my dad cry. Dads don't cry. He makes funny blubbering noises. He's not my dad. I want my dad back. I want Bapu.

My eyes water, and the room goes blurry as if the gods forgot to turn on the windshield wipers. Then I lean over and throw up. Nothing much comes out. I can't help it. My stomach hurts. I heave and heave, doubled over, and then a warm breeze touches my shoulder and a whiff of clove and sweet pipe wafts into my nose. I turn around, and there's Bapu.

CHAPTER 3

"You're a growing boy, Anu," Bapu says, clear as day. "You must remember to have supper." He squats in front of me and looks into my eyes. Bapu, in his yellow poncho, his bald head shiny, his beard damp from the rain. He grins, and a deep dimple forms in his left cheek while his left eyebrow rises. My Bapu's familiar smile.

My lips tremble and my chest fills with relief. He's here. It's really him. "Bapu!" I lunge forward to hug him.

My arms go right through empty air and I hit the floor, banging my knees. "Bapu!" He's gone, but he was here. The sweet pipe smell stays behind.

Ma reaches for me again, but I twist away, breathing fast. Dad sits with his elbows on his knees, his face buried in his hands.

"I want to see him," I burst out. "He was here. Standing

there." I point. The doctor is wrong. He can't see what's right in front of him.

He nods kindly. "Of course, you all may see him. Come with me."

We rush down the hall. The doctor shows us into a dimly lit room. The window is open a crack, letting in a wet breeze. Bapu's lying on a high bed, hands clasped over his chest. He never sleeps on his back. He sleeps on his side, with one arm hanging off the edge, and he snores with his mouth open.

I run to the bed. Bapu's face is calm. He will open his eyes, sit up and talk to me.

I touch his hand. His fingers feel cool. Ma and Dad and the doctor stand off to the side, letting me have my time with Bapu. They don't know my secret. "You can come back now," I whisper. "I saw you. You don't have to pretend."

Bapu doesn't move or breathe. Then I notice the gray tinge on his lips, his skin, and I'm so afraid, my teeth chatter.

CHAPTER 4

"Why do we have to leave him there?" I ask on the way home in the car. I'm in the back-seat. I keep flipping the ashtray lid on the armrest. "I don't want to leave him."

Everything is backward. Usually Dad drives when we're all together; today Ma drives and Dad slumps in the passenger seat.

"Just for now," Ma says. "Before we . . . before he—before arrangements are made."

"I want Bapu to come home with us," I say, flipping and flipping and flipping. I don't like that word, *arrangements*.

"Where else would you expect me to go?" Bapu says. He's sitting next to me. He's still wearing the poncho.

"Bapu!" I slide over to hug him, but the seat belt tightens across my chest, and my hands slip right through him.

"You can't actually touch me," Bapu says.

"Why not? Where did you go?"

"I'm not certain." Bapu frowns.

"You don't remember?"

"Anu, are you all right?" Ma glances in the rearview mirror.

"Best keep your voice down," Bapu says. "Or your ma will think you've gone off the deep end."

"What are you doing here?" I whisper.

"I have no idea. One minute I was lying on the bed, the next—it's unclear." He stares off blankly.

"That man, Dave, called you bin Laden." My eyes are watery again.

He reaches out but his arm goes through me. He seems as startled as I am. "Shona, not to worry. They're frightened and angry. They don't understand what's happened. Who can understand the evil of terrorists?"

"But you're not evil! He thought *you* were a bad man. You wouldn't hurt a fly—"

"He doesn't know where to send his anger, Shona. If I'd had time, I could have explained—"

"There was no time to explain. I don't want you to leave."

"Anu?" Ma says.

"I don't want to leave you either," Bapu says softly. "But—"

"Then stay."

"I'm not sure I can."

Ma glances in the mirror again. "What are you saying?"

"Nothing, Ma!"

I barely whisper. "We need to find a barred owl. And Dad's crying."

"Well, he's sad. I'm his daddy, Shona. I changed his diapers

16

and sang when he had colic." Bapu breaks into quiet song. *"Ni-ni-Baba ni-ni . . . soja Baba soja . . ."*

"You sang that to me at bedtime."

"*Soja* means sleep." Bapu begins to fade as Ma steers up our driveway. Gravel crackles under the tires. Don't go, Bapu. My eyelids grow heavier and heavier. I want to lie down. I want food. I want Bapu.

CHAPTER 5

I wake up to terrible quiet. I slept so long, the sun rose without me. Now I have a sick sense of having missed something important. I rub my eyes, my brain filled with pieces of dreams. Bapu's voice echoes in my ears: *Ni-ni-Baba ni-ni . . . soja Baba soja . . .*

He isn't singing his prayers next door. No sound comes from his room. Only the distant clink of dishes drifts up from the kitchen. Ma and Dad move around down there. They're pretending life is normal.

I get up and rush into Bapu's room. A lump rises tight and round in my throat. Ma made the bed. The covers stretch flat and uncaring across the mattress. Bapu's *chappals* lie forgotten near the door. They sag the way old sandals do, as if they're missing the weight of Bapu's wide feet. On the bureau, the bronze statue of Shiva, great god of destruction, lifts his leg in

18

dance. He's barely eight inches tall, but he holds the power of the universe. Fennel and rice form a circle of offerings at his feet. Bapu died and Shiva keeps dancing. The great god doesn't care either.

How can the room look the same? Bapu's dressing gown, draped over the chair, should tuck itself away. The sun shouldn't rise. The black-and-white picture of Bapu shouldn't smile on the bureau. Doesn't this day know that he's gone? Doesn't it miss him the way I do?

I want to believe he's in the bathroom, sitting on the toilet, reading the morning paper for two hours, but no, the bathroom door stands open. Nobody's inside. My heart dips so deep that I can't breathe.

In the bathroom, I lift the toilet seat, pee and nearly miss the bowl. There! Bapu's metal scissors for trimming his beard. They glint on the toilet tank as always. Has he been here? But my arms went through him. He can't pick up his trimmer. Will his ghost beard grow and grow, the way the sadhus' beards grow until they reach the ground?

I still smell his scented skin oil, the Mysore shampoo. His sandalwood soap sits in the dish where he always places it so neatly next to the folded facecloth. He tells me I make a mess. "You mustn't leave water in the dish, Shona," he says. "The soap turns to paste."

His white *punjabi*, the Indian shirt he wears to bed, hangs over the towel rack. I slam the toilet seat, splash water on my hands, splatter it all over the bathroom. Bapu! You can't leave everything behind. You didn't tell me what would happen to your shampoo and scissors and soap after you left us. I don't know what to do. I hope you can hear me.

I go down to the kitchen. Ma and Dad are in the dining room seated at the table, not standing at the counter eating on the run the way they usually do. They pushed Bapu's chair back into the corner, as if he's being punished. Dad piled his textbooks on the seat. My parents aren't going to work. They're both still in rumpled pajamas with their hair sticking out everywhere. Dad picks at his food. He looks like a ghost of my dad.

I slide into my chair. Ma made tea and tried to cook eggs, but they're soggy and running around on my plate.

I glance at the countertop and my heart leaps. Bapu's pipe and tobacco, next to the telephone book! His reading glasses are in the case next to the pipe. What if he needs to read? What will he do? Then my heart dives into my shoes. He can't be gone.

Dad sighs through his nose and takes a gulp of his tea. His eyes are red-rimmed, and he seems smaller, wrinkled, like a dried-up grape turning into a raisin. Our whole house feels parched without Bapu.

"What will we do with his things?" Ma asks, looking at Dad.

"Isn't it a bit early to worry about that?" Dad says. "He's been gone all of fourteen hours and ten minutes." He always speaks in numbers.

"Keep his things here," I say. He has to come for them.

"We need to pick up his clothes from the hospital," Ma says. She's always *practical*, a word I learned in school, which means "no-nonsense" and "matter-of-fact."

Dad takes a sip of tea and stares off into the backyard at Bapu's bird feeders, the chickadees pecking at the suet. Bapu must be there, hiding in the huckleberry bushes, watching.

"What about the family?" Ma asks.

Dad glances bleary-eyed at his watch. "In twelve hours or so, I'll try calling. They're all in bed now."

It's nighttime in India. When it's daytime there, it's nighttime here. The rest of Bapu's family still lives in India. He came here three years ago to be closer to us.

Ma places her hand over Dad's. "What about the memorial?"

"He was devout," Dad says.

"But we can't perform all the rituals," Ma says.

I stare at my plate, play with my food. My parents don't pray to the gods. Bapu's singing woke Ma too early on weekends, but she never complained.

"Auntie Biku will come," Dad says. "You'll see."

Auntie Biku! Bapu's younger sister. Coming here from India? I've seen pictures of her. She's a girl version of Bapu, only shorter and with long white hair.

"What about the cremation?" Ma says.

My heart drops. Dad's quiet, his face pale. I know what cremation is. They'll burn Bapu's body, scatter the ashes in a sacred place and perform many boring rituals to help his soul rise to the gods. His soul can't leave.

"You can't cremate Bapu!" I say.

"Your Bapu wanted to be cremated," Ma says. "It's tradition."

"He wanted his ashes thrown into the Twin Rivers," Dad says in a thin voice. "It's a wild place with many birds."

"Bapu doesn't want to leave me!" I shout.

Dad and Ma glance at each other.

"He told me after . . ." My voice trails off. How can I say, *after he died*?

Ma puts a hand over mine. "Anu, Bapu doesn't want anything

anymore. He's . . . sleeping. A very long sleep. A sleep that lasts forever—"

"I'm not stupid." I pull my hand back. "So, what about the boring rituals? You'll send him away!"

"We're not going to perform boring rituals. Cremation doesn't hurt him. He's already gone."

"How do you know it doesn't hurt? How can he come back if, if . . ."

"Oh, sweetie. I wish—I know you were very close to Bapu." Ma hardly ever calls me sweetie. "This is hardest on you—"

"It's not hard on me. It's not! Bapu's here."

"Of course he is." But I can tell by the sadness in her eyes that she doesn't believe me.

After breakfast, Ma drives us to the hospital. She and I wait in the car while Dad goes in. I wait and wait, sliding back and forth, kicking the driver's seat until Ma tells me to stop. "You'll knock my teeth out."

I hold my breath, let it out, but Bapu doesn't show up.

Dad comes back carrying Bapu's poncho and boots and clothes. My mouth dries up.

"I told the nurse that my father wore double socks," Dad says in the car. His voice is tight. "But they returned only one pair. Two plus two equals four, I tried to tell her. Four socks. She wouldn't listen."

I tap my fingernail on the window. Two plus two equals four. Dad thinks in equations. What does it matter how many socks Bapu wore? He's wearing ghost socks now.

"They must've lost the other pair," Ma says. She pats Dad's shoulder. "It's okay."

"It's not okay," Dad mutters, but he's silent the rest of the way.

At home, he puts everything in Bapu's room and shuts the door.

Bapu doesn't come back. I check his e-mail on my computer. Only spam. I check my e-mail in case he sent a ghost message through cyberspace. Nothing except for five e-mails from Unger, saying he's sorry about my grandfather and asking how I'm doing. I nearly forgot my best friend.

CHAPTER 6

I lie awake in bed. I pray to Garuda and count to one hundred, two hundred, three hundred and seventy-three. I keep a flashlight switched on under the covers and read aloud from *The Ramayana*, in which Rama, the boy who could shoot arrows with perfect aim, discovers he's the reincarnation of the great god Vishnu the Preserver.

I hope Vishnu will preserve my Bapu, keep him whole and real and close, even if my parents cremate him. I want to steal the statue of Shiva from Bapu's room, but I'm afraid to go back in there. Dad doesn't want anything disturbed. He and Ma argue about Bapu's trunkful of belongings, the shrine, the Shiva statue.

I stay awake in case Bapu comes back, but I fall asleep at the last minute, the way I do right before Santa squeezes down the chimney. I want to see Santa just once, but he's sneaky. One minute, the empty pillowcase lies flat at the end of my bed, the next minute it's full of gifts.

I try to stay up for Bapu, but sleep comes inky black. I wake up to Ma and Dad shouting on the telephone in the middle of the night. They're telling the Indian relatives about Bapu—Dad's uncles, cousins and second cousins. We have a million relatives.

In the morning, my flashlight and books sit neatly on the nightstand, and the covers are pulled up and tucked in. Bapu must have come while I slept.

I don't go to school for a few days. American friends file in and out of the house, bringing flowers and cookies. Big white sympathy cards with shiny patterns clutter the mantelpiece. The flowers wilt on the tables and give off sweet, rotting scents. Dad's buddies from the university, the staff at Ma's office, all bring food and say how sorry they are. A few Indian friends come, people we haven't seen in months. Cards arrive from the principal and Ms. Lumpenberger, my teacher.

Andy Howe and his parents bring a purple hydrangea in a pot. He's in my grade, but I don't hang out with him. He's always off reading by himself. A fluffy yellow wig flops on his head like a giant omelet. Everyone at school knows it's a wig. Andy has cancer.

"I'm sorry about your grandpa, Anu," he says in a squeaky voice.

"Thanks for coming, Andy. How are you doing?" I'm trying to be polite, trying not to stare at his fake hair.

"My grandpa died too. He crossed over to the other side three years ago." Andy shakes my hand with cool, frail fingers.

I pull my hand away and tuck it into my pocket. I never shake hands with friends! We slap each other on the back, punch each other in the arm. And I want to tell Andy that Bapu didn't *cross over* anywhere. He's hovering nearby, watching the parade of friends. He's probably drooling for all the food.

Andy doesn't stay long. He gets tired easily.

I thank the gods for bringing over Unger with his mom, for taking my mind off Andy's hair and Bapu for a minute.

Unger's wearing a T-shirt with an American flag printed on the front, and his thick glasses are fogged up as usual. The specs have huge black rims and take up half his face. He's carrying a stack of comics.

In my room, he drops the comics on my bed. "Did you go to India or something? How come you're not at school? I sent you a million e-mails."

"Sorry. I've been way busy." Busy looking for Bapu, watching for a sign.

Unger removes his glasses and wipes them on his T-shirt. "We have a lot of catching up to do."

We trade comics. I loan Unger *The Ramayana* and borrow *Spider-Man* and *X-Men;* then he pulls a wad of dollar bills from his pocket. "I'm selling my old baseball cards. I made seventeen more dollars this week. I can open my own bank account."

"Cool, Unger," I say, but I can't muster much interest. He's always coming up with a new business idea. His dad is an insurance salesman. Unger says he wants to be richer than his dad, live in a mansion in Malibu and drive a convertible.

"I'll be loaded when I turn eighteen." He boots up my computer and surfs the Internet for *personal finance.*

26

"I saw him," I say.

"Saw who?" He doesn't look up.

"My grandfather, after he died. But now I'm forgetting what he looked like."

Unger pushes the glasses up on his nose. "I forget what my grandma looked like. She was in a retirement home. I only saw her, like, once a month."

"Ma and Dad would never have let Bapu live in a retirement home."

Unger shrugs, clicking through to www.make-a-zillion.com. I can't imagine not seeing Bapu for a whole month. Now I might not see him for even longer. The thought carves a hollow pit inside me; the word *forever* lurks at the bottom. I won't go there. I can't go down that far.

CHAPTER 7

The following afternoon, our weird next-door neighbors, Ms. Mumu and her daughter, Izzy, bring a huge Tupperware container of homemade, oversized chocolate chip cookies. Each cookie takes up a whole plate. Ms. Mumu wears flowing skirts and crystals around her neck. Although Izzy is my age, she's giraffe-tall, skinny and pale. Who wouldn't be with a name like Izzy Mumu? Izzy is homeschooled. She wears beaded necklaces, bracelets, earrings. She probably stuffs beads up her nose.

We all sit in the living room eating cookies.

"Anu will need a place to stay after school," Dad says. "Just until Priti and I get home from work."

Ms. Mumu, breathless and heavy in her flowing dress, smiles.

"We'd love to have Anu stay with us. He and Izzy can get acquainted."

Get acquainted? A lump of cookie turns to glue in my throat.

The phone rings, and the kettle whistles at the same time. The grown-ups get up and drift into the kitchen, and I'm left staring at Izzy. She stares back at me through silvery cat eyes. I don't know if she wants to play with me, kill me or turn me into a bead on her necklace.

"Where's your TV?" she asks with a lisp, as if she has something caught between her teeth.

"My parents put it away for a while," I say. "I had nightmares about the planes hitting the towers."

"Me too, and I cry. My mom watches the news all the time. She's totally hypnotized. She bawls her eyes out."

I sigh. "I miss *The Simpsons*."

"Look at what I've got—way better than TV anyway." Izzy pulls something from her pocket and puts it on the table. I nearly jump out of my skin. It's a miniature gray head with tangled black hair. The nose is big and wide, the eyes sewn shut. "Shrunken head from Ecuador," Izzy says. "I bought it on the Internet."

"You mean it's real?" I lean forward, but I'm afraid to touch it. "It's too small to be a real head."

"Not the real one, silly. It's rubber, looks exactly like the real one. I think she was a woman. It takes years to shrink the real heads."

I glance toward the kitchen. Nobody's coming. Ma and Ms. Mumu are laughing. How could Ms. Mumu make Ma laugh? Dad's talking on the phone.

I lean forward and whisper, "You mean they actually chopped off—"

"Wild headhunters of the Amazon river." Izzy's brows rise. Her hair is so blond, her eyelashes shine silvery white. "First they take out the bones and fill the head with pebbles and sand, and then they heat the head in, um, sulfur, and other things. . . ."

"No way."

"Way. Then they shake all that stuff in the head for seven weeks and press on the skin to keep the features."

I lean back and suddenly my head feels fuzzy and I put my hands to my neck. I wonder if Izzy wants to cut off my head. I wonder if she secretly chops off heads in her room and presses them into beads around her neck. "How do you know all this?"

"I read." She leans over to whisper. "They have the real shrunken heads at the Mystery Museum on Divine Island."

"Mystery Museum? They have real heads?" A shiver runs up my spine.

"A whole bunch of other stuff too. I collect curiosities over the Internet. Www.mystery-museum.com." She gives me a toothy smile.

I never knew you could collect curiosity. I guess that since Bapu died, my family has been collecting sadness.

CHAPTER 8

The gods send rain after rain after rain. Finally the flooding lets up. Clouds still clutter the sky, and a damp wind blows, rattling leaves off the trees. Ma's gone back to work, and Dad is sleeping. He sleeps a lot these days. He brought home Bapu's ashes in an urn, but I'm not allowed to look inside. Dad keeps the urn in his room. Bapu's not in the urn, anyway. He's floating somewhere on the edge of the forest.

I make a bowl of granola and consider my options. I haven't seen Izzy since she came over. I have to go back to school tomorrow. The thought makes my stomach flip upside down, but I still have a day to find Bapu.

I dress in my bird-watching gear and slip outside. I'm afraid to get lost in the woods, so I drop seed and keep the house in view. I'm wearing my yellow poncho. The forest whispers, and I'm sure

I hear Bapu's voice, the crunch of his boots in the dirt. When I stop to listen, there's nothing but branches sighing in the wind.

I find a clearing and sit. I try not to move, but I fidget, tapping my foot. My mind drifts up into the treetops. I look for the inner light. I picture a flickering bulb inside my chest. I can't help picking up rocks, tracing the lines in the moss. I think of the sadhus in India not moving, barely breathing for twelve years. How do they do that?

I close my eyes and pray to Garuda, but nothing happens. The lonely wind cries around me, telling me to go home. I try to picture Bapu. His face grows fuzzy, and then as I'm hiking home, following my trail of seed, Bapu moves along beside me. I know he's there—a hint of his yellow poncho flashes in my vision. I can't hear his footsteps. He's silent this time and see-through, like Jell-O. "You're still here. I knew it!" I shout. I know not to hug him. I thought I'd be happier to see him. I thought all my worries would go away.

"Don't get cold, Shona," Bapu says. "Next time you come into the woods, bring a friend. Don't go off alone like this."

"You don't have to worry about me. Worry about Dad. He's sleeping too much."

"He'll be okay. Give him time."

"I have to stay with Izzy Mumu in the afternoons, and I don't want to go back to school."

"Why not? All your friends are at school. What about Unger?"

"He's really cool, but . . ." I bite my lip. My hands are clammy.

"The children have been calling you names. Osama, bin Laden . . ."

"Just a couple of kids."

32

"This is something new. You always enjoyed school."

"Things are different since . . ." I kick a clod of dirt, kick and kick.

"This too shall pass, Shona. You must talk to your father about all these things."

"I need *you*, Bapu. What do I do?" I want to hug him. A lump grows in my throat. I want him to cook, but his hand will go right through the spatula. I want him to read to me, but his hand will go right through the book.

I snap open the umbrella above our heads. He can't even hold the umbrella anymore.

"Only the gods know what you must do, Shona. I'll tell you a story that may help you decide."

I walk closer to him. My teeth chatter, and the sideways rain sneaks under the umbrella, soaking my shoes and socks. I want to feel Bapu's warmth, but he's not warm and he's made only of air.

"Umbrellas were invented in India," Bapu says. "You come from a sophisticated country. Complicated and very old, like the story of Jamadagni. He was skilled at the use of the bow. His wife, Renuka, was so devoted that she ran after every arrow he shot and picked it up."

"Like a golf caddy or the ball boy in tennis?"

"Yes, like that. One day, she ran after an arrow and did not return until nightfall. She blamed the heat of the sun for the delay."

I know the sun is very hot in India, so hot you could fry your toes into chicken nuggets.

"Jamadagni grew furious and shot an arrow at the sun."

"But the sun is so far away. Ninety-three million miles, Dad says."

33

"Indeed, the arrow traveled ninety-three million miles. The sun begged for mercy and offered another solution."

Oh. I know. I'm brilliant. "The umbrella."

"Exactly. He gave Renuka an umbrella to protect her from the heat the next time she ran after an arrow." Bapu gives me a long look. His eyes grow bright.

"That's the end of the story?" My heart sinks even farther into my boots.

"What ending would you prefer?"

"I don't get it, and I don't see what umbrellas and arrows and the sun have to do with anything at all!"

I break into a run. The rain slices in under the umbrella and washes Bapu away.

CHAPTER 9

Essay, Home and Family
by Anu Ganguli

Sarasvati is the Hindu goddess of learning and the arts. She loves trees. She
inspired the guy who built our two-story
home out of Douglas fir timbers. The
floors are wood. The outside walls are
cedar shingles. It has tall glass windows and built-in (inner) lights.

  Sarasvati is also the goddess of
drawing and music. She lugs around
sitars and drums and brought our piano.
Ma plays, but mostly she fixes stomachs.

Indian kids pray to Sarasvati when
they want to become rock stars or
artists like van Gogh. He cut off his
own ear. She can be felt in our home,
but especially in museums, or sometimes
in picture books.

But she's not helping me make sense of Bapu's umbrella tale. I'm sitting on the bouncy bus next to Unger, trying to finish my homework while we head out on an exciting field trip to the natural history museum.

The bus hits a bump, and my pen jolts across the page. Curtis keeps kicking the back of my seat. Unger presses his nose to the window, where someone pasted a sticker of the American flag.

"Hey, Anus, got any more of those humungous cookies?" Curtis shouts behind my head.

I roll my eyes. He has the vocabulary of a worm. I think anus is the only part of the body he knows.

"His name is Anu. Ah-new," Unger says, punching the seat.

"Don't even listen to him," I say, but my fingers curl into a fist. A few kids snicker; others ignore Curtis. If he weren't a human worm, he'd be the ten-headed Hindu demon, Ravana. He'd need ten heads just to make a single brain.

"Why don't you go back to Afghanistan?" Curtis says.

"Why don't you learn geography?" I say. I want to punch him in the nose.

"Anu's Indian," Unger says.

"Whatever," Curtis says. "Go back to your own country."

"I am in my own country!" My throat goes dry. I never know what to say. Last week he called me a terrorist. I don't look like a terrorist. At least, I don't think so. What does a terrorist look like? Do they all have black hair and brown eyes? Curtis was at the school assembly. He must have heard the principal say not to pick on people who look different. Bad people attacked the Twin Towers, but I am not one of them.

Now Curtis is bullying a skinny blond girl who wears home-made clothes. He takes a break from harassing her when we get to the museum. We see an exhibit that shows the West Coast millions of years ago, when volcanoes sprouted from the sea, but I can't help thinking that Izzy's Mystery Museum must be more exciting.

After school, I nearly walk all the way home before remembering that I have to go to the Mumus' house. My heart pounds. I'm afraid it will push through my ribs. I close my fingers around the house key on a string around my neck. *For emergencies*, Ma said. The metal is warm from being under my shirt.

Ms. Mumu answers the door in her flowing dress. The crystals gleam on her necklace.

"Come to the kitchen," she says. "You and Izzy can get acquainted." She wraps a big doughy arm around my shoulders. The house smells like burnt cookies and cat food. A few cats wander around. They're white with black patches. "I call them Holstein cats," Ms. Mumu says. "After Holstein cows, you know." We pass a room full of books and papers and a computer on a desk. "I'm a writer, and that's my study."

We end up in the kitchen. It's brown with green countertops, like a jungle. I sit across from Izzy and try to think about learning short division. When do I get to see the shrunken heads? When do I get to eat? The numbers on the page turn into slices of strawberry cheesecake. My mouth waters and I'm afraid I will drool. I'm in the kitchen, where the food is supposed to be. Ms. Mumu is making something. For Izzy and me, I hope, not for the cats. They wander in and out to crunch food from bowls on the floor. Ms. Mumu brings a plate of the enormous cookies.

"Made with Splenda," she says. "I'm trying to lose weight."

I devour the cookies, which are too sweet and salty. When we finish our homework, Izzy looks up at me through her silver-gray eyes. "Come and see my collection." Her lisp is strong today. She says *see* like *thee*.

On her desk next to a computer are packages of blood-red soap that stains your hands red, fish-tasting candy, plastic snot that you can stick up your nose, dirt soap that makes you dirt-ier the more you use it.

"These are cool!" I say. "Can we go to the Mystery Museum?"

"My mom took me once. You have to take two buses and then a ferry to Divine Island. I'm not allowed to go by myself."

"Ma and Dad would never let me go by myself either."

Izzy shows me key chains, magnets and pressed-penny sou-venirs, tiny totem poles and a piece of petrified coral fifty mil-lion years old. She has a box full of stones in all colors.

"The museum has a two-headed pig in a jar and the real shrunken heads in the back," she says, and shivers. "And two mummies and a magician named Karnak who can make any-thing happen. But my mom won't take me into that back room. She's afraid the mummies will scare me."

"Does she know you have the shrunken head?"

"Yeah, it's a toy. It was only two dollars and fifty cents. I sent in my allowance, and they sent me the head." She bounces on the bed. "There's a fortune-teller, Stella. She's this lady in a glass case with a big crystal ball. You put fifty cents in and she moves—her eyes even move—and she gives you your fortune." Izzy hands me a piece of cardboard inscribed with STELLA'S PROPHECIES in big letters. Below, in smaller letters, are the words "You're in luck, my friend. Fortune will soon be thine. . . ."

"Wow, cool." I desperately want Stella to tell my fortune.

Then I spot a picture of a skinny man holding a baby on his knee. He looks a lot like Izzy.

"That's my dad," she says. "He died when I was a baby. I don't remember him."

"My Bapu's—my grandfather's ghost comes back—"

"He's wandering through the ether?" Her eyes go wide.

"I don't know where Bapu goes when I don't see him."

"Bapu—what kind of name is that?"

"His real name is Siddhartha."

"Oh!" Izzy presses her hand to her mouth. "Siddhartha? He was born a Hindu but he became the supreme Buddha, the Enlightened One."

"How do you know?" Izzy's a talking encyclopedia. I wonder if she'll tell me more if I press a button in her back.

"I learn about world religions right after lunch. Your grandfather is the Buddha. If his name is Siddhartha, that is. The Buddha wandered around India until he got bored and started a new religion. Here, I'll show you." She boots up the computer and clicks onto a Web site, www.siddhartha-the-buddha.com. The serene statue of the supreme, enlightened Buddha looks like Bapu without the beard! Could it be true?

"There, that's him," Izzy says. "Siddhartha became the Buddha and reached, um, Nirvana, the supreme state . . . of . . ."

"That's why Bapu's kind of see-through?"

"Yeah! And it means he isn't really gone."

My fingers tremble. Bapu never said he was the Buddha, the Enlightened One. Maybe I was supposed to know by looking at him. Bapu is still here, everywhere, fuzzy. He's in Nirvana! I just have to get him back.

CHAPTER 10

After work, Ma changes from her white coat into baggy sweats and cooks to NPR on the radio. Sometimes the hospital smell stays on her for a while—rubbing alcohol and sickness. Dad goes to his study and shuts the door.

"Set the table, please, Anu." Ma plunks plates and forks and knives on the counter.

I take Dad's books off Bapu's chair and dump them on the floor. Then I drag the chair to the table. In his supreme state of fuzziness, Bapu needs a place to sit.

At supper, the three of us clink our dishes without a word. Ma glances at Bapu's chair, but she doesn't push it away. I work up my nerve.

"Why didn't you tell me?" I ask.

Dad glances up at me. His eyebrows rise. "Tell you what?"

"That Bapu was the Buddha."

"What gave you that idea?"

Ma's face freezes.

"Siddhartha," I say. "The Buddha was Siddhartha, the Enlightened One. He started a whole new religion. You didn't tell me."

"Who told you all this, Unger?" Ma's face is stiff.

"Izzy told me, and I saw it on the Internet. He's still here. The Buddha never dies. He's one with everything."

"Don't believe all you read on the Internet," Ma says.

"Anu, many people are named Siddhartha," Dad says gently.

"What do you mean, 'many people'? I don't know of anyone—"

"Not here. In India," Dad says. "Names are different there. Some have many syllables, like Krishnaswami, for example. Some names are difficult to pronounce. Your name, Anu, is easy. Many people have that name in India."

"I know—you told me, Dad. But I bet kids don't get called *Anus* in India."

"The kids call you Anus?" Ma's voice tightens. She glances at Dad, and he shakes his head slightly.

"Probably not," Dad says. "It's not right for kids to call you Anus. Their name-calling comes from ignorance."

"Curtis has a miniature brain," I say.

Ma presses a hand to her mouth, as if she's trying not to laugh.

"In India, they're used to the name Anu," Dad says. "Like John or Joe here."

"Then why didn't you call me John or Joe?" Suddenly I wish for the nickname Bapu gave me, Shona.

"Don't you like your full name?" Ma says. "Anurag means—"

"I know, Ma. It means love." She's told me a million times. I'll never tell my friends. *Anu-rag. Lovey-dovey.*

"Many people are named Siddhartha as well," Dad says. "The Buddha lived a long time ago. Your Bapu was just your Bapu."

No, he isn't.

"Eat the rest of your supper," Ma says.

The food thickens on my plate. "I don't want it. The potatoes are lumpy."

"Please, Anu. Not now," Ma says. "I've had a long day."

I push my plate away. I'm being terrible. I can't help it.

"I know it's difficult, Anu." Dad scratches his beard.

"Are we having *payesh* for dessert?" I ask.

"*Payesh* takes a long time to make." Ma taps her fingers on the table. She's been biting her nails again.

"Bapu always made *payesh.*"

Ma keeps tapping. "Bapu had time. He had all day to cook—"

"Bapu made the best *payesh* on earth!"

"Look, we'll get you *payesh,*" Dad says quickly, glancing at Ma. "We'll go to the Indian bakery in Bellevue this weekend."

"I want Bapu's *payesh,*" I whisper. I don't know about any Indian bakery. I don't even know where Bellevue is.

Dad and Ma stare at each other. Dad reaches out to put a hand over Ma's shaky fingers.

I need Bapu all the time, not just when he drops in. Now he's not the Buddha, and I don't know what to do.

I have to talk to Izzy.

CHAPTER
11

Since the birth of the universe, the gods hang around us, in everything and on everything and under everything. So don't kill the bugs under rocks. They're the gods. The gods also live in the air we breathe and in the key I'm trying to fit into the front-door lock.

"We can't be here too long," Izzy says. "My mom will come looking for us. Hurry up. Here, let me try." She jiggles the key and finally forces the door open. She glances around and blinks. "I keep forgetting that your house is as big as the school." She tiptoes through the quiet.

"Big, big!" I yell, waiting for the echo, but my voice rises and lodges under the skylight. Izzy yells "big, big" and we both yell until we get bored, about a minute later.

We pass Bapu's room. The wooden floor creaks beneath our feet. His door is closed. My heart pounds. I think of Shiva on the other side.

We rummage through the closet where Ma keeps the pictures. We find a box marked SIDDHARTHA GANGULI and look through the pictures.

I hope Izzy's plan works. She showed me a Web site: www.bring-back-dead-loved-ones.com. We're supposed to find the right photo and take it to the graveyard.

"But my Bapu was cremated," I say. "He's not buried. How will I find him?"

"All spirits hang out in the cemetery, around the headstones. We have to find a good picture of him."

I'm not so sure, but I'm willing to try anything. There's a picture of Bapu riding an elephant in India, another with his foot up on a log and a pipe in his mouth. In another one, he's working in his garden in Santiniketan, Bengal, India. He's standing next to Amma. I hold the picture close to my face. Izzy pulls it away. "Your eyes will get stuck like that."

I hold the picture out. A mouthful of teeth crowds Amma's smile. She has big, gentle eyes and a round face. Dad looks like her.

Izzy squints closer. "Your grandmother? She has long hair."

"I never knew her. She died before I was born."

"You could use this picture. Your grandfather had hair back then."

"He's been bald as long as I've known him." In the oldest picture we have, Bapu is already a grown-up.

She chooses a picture of Bapu and me, taken only two

45

months before. I hold the picture to the light, and my stomach squeezes and squeezes. I can't breathe, and then I remember to suck air into my lungs. Bapu stands straight and tall with his shoulders back. His hand rests on my head. I feel his touch now, and turn around.

Nothing there.

"I'll take this picture," I say.

The forgotten graveyard is three blocks west, next to a tangled forest. The sign hanging halfway off the gate reads IOLA CEMETERY. On the rusted wire fence hangs another sign, ANGLE PARKING, where tree roots push up through cracks in the concrete. On either side of the gate, somebody planted holly and maple trees a long time ago. The trees are nearly up to the power lines.

Izzy shoves the gate and it squeaks open. We enter a weird world of headstones and towering firs, maples and pines. I've never seen such huge trees anywhere, not even in the woods behind our house. The air smells of autumn leaves. A cracked road curves around the grounds and back to the gate. Robins and sparrows twitter in the trees.

Izzy and I traipse across pine needles and huge pinecones. "Anderson, James," Izzy says, reading a shiny red granite headstone. "1841 to 1909. Anderson, Henry, 1889 to 1931. Anderson, Laverne, 1898 to 1953. It's an Anderson family plot." A red-leafed bush grows from Laverne's grave. I wonder if she's inside the bush, the way the gods are in everything. Different plants grow from different graves—boxwood, Oregon grape. Bapu loved birds and plants, and he taught me the names, but I don't let on that I know. Kids at school would call me Garden Boy. Or worse, Garden Anus.

We pass many graves with different-size headstones, some so old the names and dates are worn off. Other graves have only mossy stone edging around a plot and maybe a plastic plant nearby. I feel sorry for those dead people who got plastic plants. Nobody knows who they are. I want everyone to know who my Bapu is, that he's special, that my family can't live without him.

Two graves have only white crosses. "Military," Izzy says. Some just have a stick with a typed sign. American flags flap over others.

Izzy strides to the west corner and points at a headstone. It looks new. "My daddy." She kneels. "My mom takes care of the grave." She runs her fingers along the carved name: IAN MUMU.

"Mumu was your dad's real last name?" I ask. Hard to believe he died when Izzy was a baby.

"Mom and Dad wanted to give me a first name like his, starting with *I*. So they named me Isadora, Izzy for short." She straightens up. "I love you, Daddy." She blows him a kiss. I touch the cool headstone. I can't feel Bapu here. He's not whispering in the air, not touching my shoulder.

No matter where we go in the graveyard, there's no sign of him. No Siddharthas, no Gangulis. No Krishnaswamis or Indras or Vishnus or Shivas or Lakshmis or Anus. Not a single Indian name. Like when we pass the FLOWERS-4-YOU sign that reads, "If your name is Mary, come in for a free rose." I know the sign will never read "Priti," my mom's name, or "Rijoy," my dad's, or "Bapu" or "Siddhartha" or "Anu."

The world turns blurry again, and a cold, scared feeling comes into me. The picture of Bapu isn't helping. The Web site was wrong. All the way home, I hold the photo in my pocket.

CHAPTER 12

Bapu was just here in his room, in the scent of his pipe smoke. He stepped out for a minute. He'll walk back in and tell us all to leave so he can pray. He likes to pray in private.

The Shiva shrine waits in the corner. The Great God of Destruction holds one arm up and one down in blessing and protection, while the other two arms hold a drum and a single flame from a sacred fire. How could I have found him scary? He grew big in my mind, but he's only a small statue. What scares me now is what I can't see.

Ma packs Bapu's pajamas, shirts, *kurtas, chappals,* boots and pants into boxes. Bapu can't take care of his things now. Ma can give them to Goodwill or Auntie Biku when she comes, and his belongings are helpless.

I open the window and let in the air from the woods. My scalp tingles in the breeze. I feel Bapu's fingers brush my hair.

Ma works steadily, folding clothes, a determined look on her face. I sit cross-legged in front of Shiva and press the palms of my hands together in prayer, the way I saw Bapu do a million times. What does the prayer pose do? Can the gods see my hands, like a lighthouse from the sea? Can they stop Bapu from leaving?

Ma stops folding behind me. I feel her watching me. She never prays. Bapu's singing always jolted her awake too early. But just before dawn, when the sky is still new, Bapu said, the gods come closest. You can almost touch them.

I speak to Bapu in my mind, and Ma keeps folding. She's decided not to talk to me now. I know she's figuring out what to say.

"Anu, Auntie Biku will be here soon," she says finally. "She'll sleep in this room."

My legs go numb. "But this is Bapu's room."

Ma pauses. "She's his very dear sister. Bapu would want her to sleep here."

I slump onto the bed. I'm sorry, Bapu. Sorry I couldn't stop them from cremating you. Sorry you can't keep your room. Where are you now? Floating up near the ozone layer?

When Dad gets home, I hear him fixing a snack, and then he helps Ma yank the sheets off the bed.

"Will you give the statue to Biku?" Ma asks Dad.

"Can you leave Shiva here?" I ask. "Bapu prayed to Shiva. He taught me all about the gods. They're everywhere."

Ma and Dad trade glances, and then Dad sits next to me on the newly made bed. He puts an arm around my shoulders. He smells of spicy aftershave, not like Bapu. "Anu, you can decide to be anything you want—Christian, Hindu, Buddhist, atheist. We've taught you about all religions so that, eventually, you can make up your own mind. Maybe you don't understand what I'm telling you now. Whatever you choose to believe, it's six of one and half a dozen of the other."

There he goes with the numbers again. "Didn't you ever pray to Shiva?" I ask.

Dad shakes his head. "I left for boarding school when I was very little. I never prayed with your Bapu. He was stuck in the old days. Old days and old ways."

"The gods never get old!"

"I'm just telling you to think for yourself," Dad says.

"I am thinking for myself. I always think for myself. You want to forget Bapu. That's all. You don't want him anymore. You're giving away everything. You burned him. He won't even know where to sleep, or where he lived, or anything!"

"That's not true," Dad says, his voice breaking. "Bapu is always with us, but not in his clothes and his statue. He's in our memories."

I swallow, my throat dry. My chest aches, as if someone dropped a Massive Stroke on it. Is Bapu hiding in my memory? I remember him and remember him, but our moments together are fading. I don't want to forget.

Ma and Dad carry Bapu's things into the garage.

I stay awake late, wait forever for Ma and Dad to go to bed. Then I tiptoe to the hallway. The kitchen clock ticks and the refrigerator buzzes. The light's off in my parents' room, and Dad's soft snores drift from under the door. I tiptoe through the house. The floor groans underfoot. I stop and wait, my

51

heart thudding. Then I keep going. The garage door squeaks. I take about a year to open it, then another year to shut it behind me.

I gulp, turn on the light and search through the boxes. The Shiva statue hides at the very bottom of one, wrapped in a *kurta*. I steal Shiva and then stuff all the clothes back into the boxes. A sleeve sticks out here and there. I'm not good at being neat.

I tiptoe back to my room and keep Shiva next to me under the covers. Outside, the rain falls in sheets, *tap-tap*ping on the roof and gutters. The rain has been falling so steadily for days, without a breath in between, that you start to believe there was never a sunny day, that there will never be another.

CHAPTER

13

Bapu visits my dreams.

He shows up on our doorstep with a suitcase, as if he's arriving from India instead of from the heavens. Relief floods through me. My happiness spills out. He didn't die. He wasn't burned. Here he is, the way he was, except he looks strange wearing a white *dhoti punjabi*, the long shirt and baggy Bengali pants. Somewhere between earth and the gods, he got rid of the poncho.

"You're here for good! I knew it!" I shout, glancing in triumph at the suitcase, but Bapu shakes his head. He shimmers like a mirage as he steps into the house. He hands me a yellow daisy. "From your garden. Spring is coming—"

"But it's fall!"

"Spring will come eventually. I can't stay long. I've only come to tell you—"

"What do you mean, you can't stay long? Why not?" My lungs squeeze and squeeze.

"I can't keep dropping in. You've got other dreams waiting. Your friends Unger and Izzy. Birds and baseball and all that."

"No, Bapu. I want to be with you."

"I'm not long for this place. You know that, Shona."

My happiness hardens into stone in my chest. "What do I do, Bapu? Auntie Biku's coming. Dad and Ma packed your things—but I kept Shiva! I hid him in my top drawer."

Bapu frowns. "Not a good place for a most powerful god, is it? Swimming around in your undershirts?"

"I have to hide him, or Ma and Dad will send him to Goodwill, or Auntie might take him to India. I'm afraid they're going to throw your ashes away and forget all about you—I'm scared." There, I've said it. The stone inside me is . . . *fear.* So many terrible pictures pushing up from blackness—Bapu and me in the woods, the sky so quiet, too quiet. Bapu falling, people falling, buildings falling, and ashes and explosions shoving at the edge of my mind. I clutch the crumpled daisy in my palm.

Bapu opens the suitcase and pulls out a golden book. Elephants dance across the cover, blocking out my dark thoughts.

"Whoa—what's that?" My jaw drops open. I've never seen moving pictures on a book. Then I remember that I'm dreaming. Anything can happen in dreams. I want to stay in this dream with Bapu forever.

"You're running out of stories, Shona," he says. "So I've brought one to help you." He opens the book and the pictures come to life in brilliant colors. An Indian marketplace, merchants selling silk and silver and vegetables and fruit. Women, men, children, dogs and cows rush through the scene and disappear. Shouts and laughter, the squeaks and clatter of carts and rickshaws fill my ears. I smell burning cow dung and incense.

"There—the story is about this man." Bapu points to a thin man wearing a *dhoti* and carrying a cane. "He believed God was in everything, and he did not question it, and then—" Bapu turns the page. A great rumbling rattles my teeth, and an elephant crashes onto the page. "He saw a rogue elephant pulling a cart, stampeding through the marketplace. The driver of the cart kept yelling, 'Get out of the way!' but the man did not listen. Since God is in everything, he believed the elephant could not hurt him. But the elephant crashed into him and threw him into the gutter, where he landed bruised and battered."

I'm watching the events unfold as Bapu turns the pages.

"A holy man came to him and said, 'Why did you not get out of the way?'

"The man explained—if God is in everything, how could God allow the elephant to hurt him? He was disappointed and disillusioned.

"Then the holy man said, 'Don't you know? If God is in everything, he is also in the driver who told you to get out of the way.'"

Bapu closes the book.

"What does it mean, Bapu?" But I think I know. He told me this story before.

Bapu winks at me, and then he's gone and I'm lying in bed in the rising light of morning. The dream—Bapu, the book, his voice—fades so quickly, and my real world rushes in from all sides. I press my eyes shut and try to bring Bapu back. Please, please. I try to fall asleep again, but the birds twitter outside in the soft rain. The darkness, the colors and sounds of my dream, are slowly disappearing. I'm clutching the dream daisy in my fist, but when I open my fingers, my hand is empty.

CHAPTER
14

We're going to the Indian bakery in Bellevue. Dad is driving again, while Ma reads all the way to the ferry. I stare out at the American flags sprouting everywhere—on store windows, lawns and cars. I wait for Bapu, but he doesn't drop in, not even when the ferry crosses churning black-blue waters.

In the bakery, I blend into a sea of dark heads. I can't help staring. Everyone in here has brown skin. Some men have turbans and beards. It's as if all the Indians in the world gathered here for sweet *gulab jamin*, *jelabis* and *barfi*, an Indian dessert sometimes covered with a thin layer of silver. You actually eat the silver, and your insides become richer.

Half the bakery is a video store featuring Hindi films I've

never heard of. The actors and actresses are all Indian, usually with fierce or romantic expressions on their faces.

The other half of the store is a long glass case filled with cakes and sweets. There's a lot of waving and shouting going on, mostly in languages I don't understand. Dad stands at the case, hands shoved into his pockets. Ma went next door to the Indian grocery, although I don't know what she plans to buy, since Bapu did all the Indian cooking. Ma never has time.

"What do you want, Anu?" Dad asks.

"*Payesh.*"

An Indian girl behind the counter comes up and asks, "Can I help you?" in an American voice. She's wearing jeans and a *kurta*. She's chewing gum. She's a few years older than me. Where did she come from? Are there more Indian kids in Bellevue? Why do they hang out here instead of where I live, on the other side of the water?

"Do you have *payesh*?" Dad asks.

She shakes her head. "You could check over at Taj Mahal restaurant, about four blocks down."

I'm staring at the multicolored cakes in the glass case, and my mouth waters.

"Do you want to go there, Anu?" Dad asks.

"I want some of these." I press my fingers to the glass.

"Okay, you choose which ones."

The girl brings a big empty box that we will fill with desserts! I grin at Dad, and he grins at me. I haven't seen him smile in a long time. His shoulders relax and his face lights up and looks totally different.

Then, in Hindi, he asks the girl something. I recognize the sharp edges of the words, but I can't understand. She nods and replies in Hindi. When we go outside, Ma is standing there holding a huge bag of groceries. Her eyes shine with excitement. "I didn't realize they had the high-quality basmati rice. And I found good saffron!"

We drive to a park by the lake and eat our sweets while watching white ducks waddle near the shore, pecking for scraps of bread. We eat and eat, and Ma and Dad don't tell me to stop, until I'm full and giddy with sugar. I nearly forget that Bapu hasn't dropped in, that his ashes wait in the urn at home, that Auntie Biku is coming all the way from India to scatter them to the sacred wind.

CHAPTER 15

At the airport, Dad and I wait in line at the security area. The officers are talking to a man in a turban, a Sikh. "I bet they think he's Osama bin Laden," I whisper to Dad. "The medic thought Bapu was Osama too. He didn't even wear a turban! Can we help that man?"

Dad's jaw tightens. "There's nothing we can do."

The security people lead the Sikh away, around the corner. He walks upright and proud, carrying a suitcase.

I keep kicking the floor. Nothing we can do, nothing we can do. I want to do something. Anything.

"Where did they take him?" I ask Dad. I already know what they're doing. They're *interrogating* him. I learned the word in class—it means grilling somebody with questions.

"They don't understand Sikhs, Anu. They're afraid, and they're ignorant. One must never underestimate the power of fear."

I notice people glancing our way. The fear slithers all around me. We're at the end of the line. The blue-haired woman in front of us turns and wrinkles her nose. Maybe I stink, but I didn't fart. Or maybe she's like Curtis at school; she thinks we're terrorists here to blow up the airport.

Then the Sikh man comes out and stands right behind us in line.

"They give you a hard time?" Dad asks.

"Nothing I haven't experienced before," the man says with a funny British accent. He shakes hands with Dad. "Parvinder Singh." Hair grows from interesting places on his face—on his cheekbones, from his nose. His eyebrows have grown together into a single bushy line.

"Rijoy Ganguli," Dad says. "This is my son, Anu."

Mr. Singh nods at me. "You off to India?"

"My aunt's coming," Dad says. "My father recently died."

"I am sorry," Mr. Singh says. "I'm off to India. My mother is ill. Otherwise I would not travel so soon after—"

"Of course. Neither would we," Dad says.

My legs go numb. *My father. Recently died.* My stomach dips with a sick, sinking feeling. The words are final, as if Dad is closing the door on Bapu.

Mr. Singh and Dad stare ahead. I can't stand waiting in line. I walk back and forth, slide from side to side.

"Anu, calm down." Dad puts a hand on my arm.

I'll never be still. I think of what Bapu said in the woods. I must learn to be silent, to listen the way the holy men do.

"Eager to meet your aunt, eh?" Mr. Singh asks, winking at me. "I have a son a few years older than you."

"Does he wear a turban too?" I ask.

"Of course."

"Do some kids—"

"Mistake him for a Muslim?" He pauses, pulls on his beard. I know his hair has grown long under the turban. I bet he ties his hair up in a bun to keep it from falling everywhere. "Of course. One kept calling him Mohammed, Mohammed, but rather than shout back, my son explained his religion, the ideals of oneness with God, the message of equality and peace for all."

"What did they say?" I can barely breathe.

Dad's frowning.

"They understood," Mr. Singh says. "They told him it was a pity most people did not understand the fine message of his religion."

"Pity he was forced to explain," Dad says.

I wonder if Mr. Singh is telling the truth. I can't imagine a bully understanding any "fine message." Could I explain anything to Curtis? How much information can he fit in his worm-brain?

The wrinkle-nosed woman turns again. "You're brave to wear your turban, young man. With all the anxiety!"

Young man? Mr. Singh must be at least forty. "I've been honored to wear this turban for many years," he says, holding his head high. "Throughout history people have fought and *died* for the right to wear it. I will not take it off now."

The woman purses her lips. "Well, you're very brave." She turns ahead again, and the line begins to move, finally. I glance sidelong at Dad. He looks Indian, but he whistles "American Pie" in the shower and reads the Seattle newspaper in the morning. My dad is not what anyone calls him. My dad is just my dad. Is it brave to be what you are, I wonder? Brave to just be yourself?

CHAPTER

16

After we get through security, the Sikh man walks away to his gate. Then we wait some more, until I see Bapu striding toward us—same long nose, same eyes, same dimple! Only he's a woman with long gray hair, hitching up her sari as she runs, wheeling a house-sized blue suitcase behind her. Auntie Biku!

She keeps smiling at me—she's covered with wrinkles—and smiling and smiling while she squeezes Dad and pinches his cheeks and wraps me in a tight hug that smells of sandalwood and mothballs. She takes my face in her hands. "How you've grown, so handsome. The family resemblance!" Her eyes go watery as she turns to Dad.

On the ride home, I can't stop staring at Auntie's profile, so much like Bapu's—only her jaw is softer and she's shorter than him. A strange hope gathers in my chest. If she's Bapu's sister, she must know secrets about him. The questions pile up in my head, but she and Dad are too busy discussing people I've never heard of.

At least I got to stay up to come to the airport. I can't wait to tell Unger. His mom makes him go to bed early. Nobody cares that I'm not in bed on time, but my mind buzzes with late-night fuzz. The questions float out and whiz away. I lean back against the seat and my eyelids droop. When I fall asleep, I'm in the forest. Water drips from the trees, and the cool air smells of pine and cedar. Bapu crouches beside me, and I try to touch him but I can't move. He says I have to remember the shimmer in everything, to listen and watch, and then he topples over on his stomach, and I'm running and I can't find my way home.

I wake up heavy with sleep, still in the car, nearly home. Empty air pushes in around me.

I stay close to Auntie Biku as we go inside.

"Such a lovely home, and so large!" she exclaims. A hint of Bapu's voice hides inside her words. I have to get him back before I forget his voice, the smell of his clothes, the way he saved baby birds when they fell from their nests.

Ma's waiting inside. While we were gone, she made Indian food—the aromas of curry and samosas fill the air—and she's even playing Indian music. A twangy melody with tabla drums flits in the background.

The house behaves itself. There isn't a speck of dust anywhere, and Ma looks neat and tidy too. She's wearing a *kurta* over jeans, like she just now remembered to be Indian. She and Auntie Biku hug, and Dad wheels the suitcase to Bapu's room.

I nearly yell "Wait!" but maybe it's good to have Auntie in

Bapu's room. Maybe she can help bring him back. As she follows Dad into the room, a new thought comes to me. What if Auntie Biku has seen Bapu too? I have to ask her, but I need to lie in bed for just a minute first.

When I wake up, still in my crumpled clothes, I'm under the covers and it's morning. The sun throws sparkles of light across the walls. A soft singing drifts in under my door.

Bapu, singing his prayers! I throw off the covers and dash into the hall. Auntie Biku's coming out of the bathroom, a cup of tea in her hand. Her voice unfurls in ribbons of song, a high, sweet version of Bapu's. She looks thin in a long white *kurta*.

Ma and Dad are talking in the kitchen, and the smells of toast and sweet *cha* drift into my nose. Usually, Ma makes Lipton tea from teabags, but not today.

"Ah, Anu, come," Auntie says. "I have to show you something." I'm in Bapu's room again, but it all looks different. The open suitcase takes up the whole floor, with clothes and books everywhere and the smell of Auntie. The only thing the same are her *chappals*, which she slips off her feet inside the door, the way Bapu did. But her sandals are smaller than his, with a thin strap over the toe instead of a fat one.

"Come, sit." She pats the bed and I sit beside her, and she opens a pink photo album.

"Your Bapu when he was a young man." There he is, standing with Auntie Biku and Amma; and again, in college with other men in uniforms. Auntie explains all the pictures and tells me who the people are.

I don't understand the family connections, all twisted like pretzels. I'm staring at a brown teenager with buckteeth, short hair plastered to his head, a striped shirt and polka-dot pants.

"Here's your second cousin Prem. He's all grown now, studying film in Mumbai." Auntie sighs. "Here's your Bapu again in university. Great cricket player and a hit with the ladies. Your Amma was lucky to get him. He loved her so." She sniffs, her nose red. "When he was very young, he loved to play crocodile with me. You jump from one bed to the other without letting the crocodiles get you. The floor is the moat. We would push the beds close together. . . ." Her voice trails off, and she stares at the wall.

I see Bapu as a kid, jumping from one bed to the other. I want to tell Auntie Biku that I saw Bapu in the hospital, in the woods. Will she think I'm crazy?

"Here, he's only a month old." She shows me a faded picture of a woman with toffee-smooth skin and long, black hair. She's wearing a silk sari, and on her lap sits a jolly baby with sagging cheeks.

"That's your ma? That's Bapu? He was chubby!" I can't imagine he ever had rolls of fat. I can't imagine he gurgled and pooped in his diaper and ate soft baby food and lost his teeth and grew a whole new set. All for what? Now he's gone.

Auntie Biku gives me that funny look again, as if she is looking through me at the past. "Our ma died young," she says. "Your Bapu became quite close to his *ayah*. You know what an *ayah* is? Like a nanny. She was a second mother to him. I was more independent, not so much in need of an *ayah*, although I was four years younger than Bapu. But in India, we spoil the boys! She doted on him, cooked his favorite desserts and took him shopping and played with him in the garden, until he grew old enough to go to school. Even then, she was like his mother. Our father never remarried. We had many aunties close by.

But—" She looks at me and her eyes brim with tears. She holds my face in her hands and says something in Bengali, shaking her head all the while.

"I saw him," I blurt. "Sometimes he talks to me."

Auntie lets go of my face and wipes the tears from her cheeks. "Of course he does." She does not sound surprised. "I dream of him too. All the time."

"He gave me a daisy in a dream."

"Bapu was very generous, Anu. Here's something else he would want you to have." She rummages through her suitcase and brings out a bigger photo album, frayed at the edges. But when she opens it, I see it's not a photo album but a stamp album full of colorful, shiny stamps like jewels.

"For me?" I can hardly speak.

"You must take great care of this—passed down through generations. Belonged to your Bapu."

My Bapu. I leaf through the pages. Several stamps are stuffed into pockets on the cover, and some extra copies of stamps are in special pockets attached to the pages. I never knew Bapu collected stamps!

I sit on the couch and tap my foot on the floor. My knee moves up and down so fast, I could have a nervous tic. Auntie sifts through her suitcase again, brings out a VHS tape and puts it on the bureau. "Family video shot by your cousin Prem, to show all of you. He never turns off the bloody camera. We'll watch it later."

We have an old VHS player in the garage, but I don't know if it works. We watch DVDs, but I don't say anything. I don't want Auntie to feel bad. Dad said India is still behind us in some ways. This must be one way.

I go to my room and hide the stamp album under my pillow. At breakfast, Ma and Dad and Auntie Biku remember Bapu. His loud singing, his love of birds, his pipe smoke, the way he read the newspaper backward, the last page first. The best stories are hidden, he always said.

A lump sticks in my throat. I can't breathe, can't talk about what I remember. The wind will suck the memories from my mouth and whisk them away forever.

"Ate ten eggs at once," Auntie Biku is saying, and everyone laughs.

"Always boiled eggs when I was little," Dad says. He's smiling, but his eyes shine with tears.

"You should've hired him as the family cook!" Ma says.

"God knows he would've been better than our cook, who burned everything," Dad says.

They fall into Bengali—I understand only a few words here and there. Where will I find my answers? In the stamp album? In Auntie Biku? I feel as though Bapu is here, closer to me although I can't see him. I miss him with a sharp ache.

Outside the window, a nuthatch pecks at the suet that Bapu hung from a tree branch. A new idea sprouts in my brain.

"Auntie," I say, tugging on her sleeve.

"Anu, you're interrupting!" Ma gives me a warning look.

"It's okay, Priti. What is it?"

"Will you go bird-watching with me?"

"Anu, it's been raining," Ma says.

"We have ponchos." I'm already out of my chair.

Ma shakes her head. "Anu, Auntie's only just arrived—"

"Nah, nah. It's all right." Auntie winks at Dad, or maybe she has dust in her eye. "Sounds like great fun."

"What about finishing your breakfast?" Ma says, turning my plate around. She has a habit of doing that, turning my plate so the food on the other side moves closer to me. Half a piece of toast grows soggy on the edge.

"I'm full up to here," I lie, pointing to my chin, and run for my bird-watching gear.

Bapu's poncho goes down nearly to Auntie's ankles, but she smiles as we head out into the woods. I go first, and this time, her breathing is louder than mine, and sniffly. Maybe she picked up a Massive Cold on the plane from India.

"This is where Bapu and I went to watch for barred owls," I explain. I feel old and important leading the way.

"I thought owls came out only at night!" Auntie shouts. Why can't she stay quiet, like Bapu?

"Some owls come out in the daytime too." Doesn't she know this? Bapu knew—*knows*—everything.

"Your Bapu was quite the bird-watcher, even in India—oh, what brambles!" Auntie clucks her tongue behind me. She's so loud, she sounds like a lost elephant stampeding through the jungle. I try to find the clearing where Bapu and I sat the last time, but the sticks and rocks and trees all begin to look the same. I choose a spot and Auntie plunks down beside me.

"We have to be very quiet to look for a barred owl," I whisper, training the binoculars on a huge fir trunk in the distance.

"A whatsit?" Auntie says in her normal voice. You can't use a normal voice in the woods—it sounds three sizes too loud. The leaves quiver.

"A barred owl," I whisper. "They can hide in plain sight, sometimes right against a tree."

"A whatsit type of owl?" she says, even more loudly.

"Patience, Auntie," I say, although my foot taps the ground. I told her three times about the barred owl. Doesn't she know about birds?

"You sound like Bapu." She pats my head. Maybe Auntie doesn't know how to whisper, the way I don't know how to whistle. Or maybe her eardrums stayed back in India, sunbathing where the weather is warm, and she can't hear herself shout. She's sitting so close, but I miss Bapu's smell.

I hold my breath, waiting for him. He has to come back now that Auntie is here with me. If he had trouble hearing me calling him, he'll have no trouble now that Auntie is yelling. But nothing happens.

"Cold in these woods, nah?" She pulls the poncho tight around her.

She's right. Fall swerved in toward us, blowing chilly air down from Alaska. In the Northwest, one minute it's summer, the next it's fall. "By Halloween, we could go below freezing," I say.

"The weather is like Darjeeling. And smell the woodsmoke." She turns her nose up to the air, and in that instant, a hint of Bapu glimmers inside her. Then he's gone.

CHAPTER
17

Ma makes popcorn while Dad puts Auntie's tape into the VHS player. He spent two hours trying to hook it up to the TV; his curses still ring in my ears. Auntie didn't seem to notice. She spent the afternoon reading to me from *The Ramayana,* and now she's making a fancy Bengali dinner. The smells of cardamom, turmeric and coriander fill the house. Bapu taught me the names of those spices.

The VHS tape whirs to life, and cousin Prem sticks his face right into the camera. He looks way older than he did in the picture, but his buckteeth and glasses hung around for the long haul. "And now, for your viewing pleasure," he shouts in a thick Bengali accent, "I bring you Auntie Biku's sixty-fifth birthday!" He sweeps the jumpy camera around a room full of brown-skinned, black-haired strangers. Aunts in saris, children running around, men laughing together. I try to imagine Curtis making fun of every last brown person there, calling even the tiniest baby Osama bin Laden. He'd have to yell his lungs out.

"Say hello, everyone!" Cousin Prem says, and everybody waves. "Hello, Uncle Rijoy, Auntie Priti, Anu!"

"Hello!" I yell, then clamp a hand over my mouth.

"This is Auntie Biku's flat in Alipore, Kolkata, first floor," Prem says, breathing loudly. "Artsy shot number one." The camera points at the fan turning lazily on the ceiling, then sideways at the doorway, then tapes the relatives talking upside down. I'm getting dizzy.

The camera bounces and jiggles out onto the balcony, zooms in on a beetle. "Artsy shot two," Prem says. "Across there is the street." Auntie's voice shouts in the background, "Where are you going, Prem?"

The camera angles in on a light-brown lizard clinging to the wall. "Gecko," Prem narrates, "the house lizard of India." Then the camera moves sideways to point at cracks and stains in the walls. "Water damage à la monsoon," he says.

"Hey, Prem!" a voice shouts from inside. "You filming mosquitoes again?"

"Or house flies?" someone else says, and laughs.

"My family does not understand art," Prem mutters. The camera pans across a courtyard dotted with palm trees. A woman rushes by in a shiny sari and flashy gold jewelry. She lifts the end of her sari over her face and giggles. Children run by, shouting, their hair slicked back and black kohl rimming their eyes. They don't have Curtis to bully them, and not even a notion that Oyster Cove exists. I want to reach through the camera and touch them. I can't help feeling that Prem's camera is about to show me something important.

"Too artsy, this boy." Auntie's sitting wedged between Ma and Dad on the couch. She munches loudly on popcorn and giggles as the video bounces outside, goes black, and then suddenly angles into a busy street where the air is thick with smoke and exhaust. Horns beep. The road chokes with bulbous white cars and scooters. Crowds of barefoot children run up to the camera and stare. I sit back, startled. Those faces come so close, looking right into me. If I didn't wash my hair or change my clothes for a month, I might look like them.

"This, the real Kolkata!" Prem bounces the camera along a crowded road. I feel like I'm on a roller coaster. I might hurl.

"A group of people gathers at the corner. We'll see what they're up to, shall we?" Prem's walking, but the camera accidentally points up to the murky sky, then sideways, filming garbage and cracks in walls, and animals crossing dusty roads. Then the camera drops to the crowd.

"What's going on there?" I ask.

"They're asking the sadhu for healing," Auntie says. "Very strange, those sadhus. Holy men, you know."

"A sadhu!" I nearly shout. A holy man! "Did he meditate in a cave for twelve years?"

Ma laughs. "They think they can heal people with a mere touch of a feather."

"Not any feather," Auntie says. "Peacock feather."

"What does the feather do?" I ask.

Auntie shrugs. "The sadhus do strange things for no reason.

74

Some stand for years with one arm up in the air. Or sit in dark caves."

"Have you heard of Ludkan Baba?" Dad asks. "He rolled thousands of miles."

"Acha," Auntie says. "Sadhus think they can do anything—banish demons, talk to the dead, and even bring them back. The feather is supposed to bring you closer to the gods."

The camera swings through the crowd and catches the edge of a brown-skinned man sitting cross-legged on a mat.

"Is that him?" I ask.

"That's the boy-Baba," Auntie says.

I'm so close to the TV, I could fall in. "So the holy man—the boy-Baba—has special powers?"

Auntie snorts through her nose. "He recites mantras—opening channels to the spirits, one supposes."

"How does he open a channel?" I hardly dare hope.

"When he renounced his old life, leaving behind all earthly possessions, he shaved off all his hair."

"Now he lets his hair grow as a tribute to Shiva," Dad cuts in. "Very strange, nah?"

"Bapu prayed to Shiva too," I say.

"Bapu was not a sadhu," Ma says.

"Be careful of sadhus," Auntie Biku says. "They're dangerous. In the fourteenth century, they were known as magicians who could fly or even live on air."

Flying, like Garuda! Could this be my answer? In the traveling sadhu who might be able to fly? A lick of fire races through me. Bapu's stories burn in my mind—the stories of the holy men, the wanderers who seek the Inner Light. They wander hundreds of miles and accept only alms and water, and sometimes cigarettes. They meditate and perform good deeds to find a direct route to holiness. They take the commuter lane without all the traffic and extra exits.

Cousin Prem's camera breaks through the crowd and there's the sadhu in a red loincloth. I suck in a sharp breath.

"He's a follower of Shiva," Auntie says. "Why Prem is filming this, I don't know!"

Prem's voice whispers, "He's a young sadhu. He carries Shiva's trident of destruction attached to a golden, two-sided drum of creation. In his other hand, he holds a long peacock feather, which he uses to anoint people with holiness."

The boy-Baba is not much older than me. A tangle of long, knotted hair tumbles down in dreadlocks. Bright eyes pierce the camera as if he can see right into me. As if he knows all my secrets.

He *is* looking at me. His mouth moves. Did he say *Anu?* I imagine I'm there, in India, the crowd parting to let me step forward. Now I'm so close, I could touch him. My fingers shake and my heart pounds.

The sadhu reaches toward me, and I'm trapped in his gaze. He swats the camera—swats *me*—with the feather. He's blessing me with holiness, and a weight lifts from my shoulders as the camera shuts off.

This is a sign.

CHAPTER

18

Auntie Biku's visit falls into a haze. Did she leave only yesterday? Did we take the boat out onto the Twin Rivers at twilight? Did she and Dad sing ancient, strange songs in Bengali, their voices rising and falling at exactly the same moments? Did Dad cry? Did Auntie Biku open the urn and send Bapu's ashes into the calm water, lapping and rippling in a soft lullaby? I can't imagine that I was ever there, reaching my hand out into the air, grasping for Bapu. I knew that when the ashes melted into the river, Bapu would not vanish. I still feel him at the edge of my mind, just around the corner.

But he doesn't show up when Izzy and I traipse out into the woods. I'm carrying the Shiva statue. Shiva has 1,008 names, each for a different part of his personality. I'd hate to see his birth certificate. I bet Indian kids have to memorize his names, the way we have to memorize the state capitals. Lucky we have only fifty states.

Shiva doesn't only destroy—he also creates new life. Bapu said one can't be separated from the other. Life from death, death from life. Where fire scorches the ground, new baby trees will grow.

Shiva's favorite method of destruction is his inner spirit of fire blazing from his third, all-seeing eye. His left eye is the moon, his right eye is the sun, and the third eye sits smack in the middle of his forehead, making him look like an alien from the planet Gorgon.

"I don't get why you want to become a holy boy," Izzy says.

"Boy-Baba," I say. "I've been anointed." I touch my cheek. I swear I can still feel the sadhu's feather brushing my skin.

We drop birdseed and Izzy marks the trees with chalk so we can find our way back. In a clearing, we set up a shrine on top of a pillowcase, beneath the overhanging branches of a huge fir tree.

"This will be *our* Shiva temple," Izzy says, and helps me arrange the offerings around Shiva—apples and cooked rice and bits of leftover, stale sweets from the Indian bakery.

I sit cross-legged in front of Shiva. Izzy sits beside me and plunks the shrunken head on the pillowcase.

"Shiva doesn't eat heads!" I cry.

"How do you know? Maybe he likes eating people too." She straightens the hair on the shrunken head.

"He doesn't! You ruined everything." I snatch the head and throw it. Then I get up and stomp back through the woods.

Izzy rushes to pick up the head and runs after me. "You're just angry because your Bapu isn't coming back, Anu."

The hollow pit opens inside me again. "You don't offer shrunken heads to Shiva!"

"I'm sorry, Anu. I was just trying to help."

I stop and lean against a tree. "I know. I still need your help, but no shrunken heads, okay?"

"Are you sure you know what you're doing?" Izzy follows me into my parents' room. "Shouldn't you be doing homework?"

Jasmine perfume tints the air, and the puffy quilt lies crumpled in an unmade heap on the bed. I trip over Dad's huge shoes.

"I'll do homework later," I say. "This is more important. You have to get the back of my head."

"I don't know how to shave. My mom doesn't even shave her legs."

"I know, and she grows a bleached mustache too," I say soberly. "I've never shaved either. I've watched my dad."

"Watching isn't the same as doing. I thought the sadhus let their hair grow long, anyway."

"First they give up their past lives. I have to give up my past hair."

Izzy stops in the middle of the room. "Does that mean you're giving me up too? Because if it does, I'm not sure I want to help."

"You can be part of my new life."

"Thanks. I'm *so* grateful." She's grinning, but I stay serious.

"You're welcome." A curious feeling shimmers inside me, a sense of knowing that this is the right thing to do. The sadhu looked me in the eye. Soon I will have the ability to bring Bapu back.

"Can your parents be part of your new life?" Izzy asks.

"They have to be. I can't live outside."

"Why not? Didn't you say the sadhus live outside in India? The rolling man—doesn't he roll everywhere, rain or shine?"

"He has disciples and people helping him. They move sharp objects out of the way. I don't have disciples."

"Still, you're cheating by staying inside."

"I'm working on it, Izzy. Give me time."

"What about your parents? What will they say when they see your shaved head?"

I push the bathroom door and it squeaks open, revealing a blue sink, toilet and tub, like an aquarium with a skylight. I stand there with my hand against the door. I hadn't thought about what Ma and Dad would say. I can't worry about that now. My calling comes from a higher place. "They'll yell at me. I'll have to deal with it."

"What if they ground you?"

"They've never done that."

"What if they spank you?"

"My parents have never spanked me, not even once."

Izzy sticks out her bottom lip. "Mom spanked me when I stayed out after dark and she had to call the police. I was just digging for worms, so I think shaving your head qualifies for spanking."

"Shaving my head to become holy doesn't count." Besides, all

I care about is getting Bapu back. I've watched Dad shrivel from sadness. His Amma died a long time ago, and now Bapu. How will we live without him?

I glance up at the skylight high above. For now, the bathroom is my temple. "Hurry up, Izzy. My parents will be home in half an hour."

"Okay! 'Cause Mom will notice we're gone before that."

I glance in the mirror. I don't look serene and wise. I look . . . scared.

Izzy sits on the fuzzy toilet-seat cover. "This isn't a good idea. What if you cut yourself and bleed everywhere?"

"It's an electric razor with a safety guard on it. Dad says it cuts a millimeter from the skin."

"So, now you're an expert."

I wonder if Izzy feels bad about not having a dad. She can't watch him shave. My dad shaves every day and drops a number into every conversation. A millimeter, a centimeter, or ninety-three million miles.

I rummage in the cabinet. Where is the razor? I pull off the top of the deodorant bottle. The sharp scent nearly knocks me over. "Can you believe grown-ups spread this stuff on their armpits?"

"To keep from stinking," Izzy says. "When you grow up, you start to smell bad. You ripen, like cheese. If grown-ups didn't wear deodorant, we'd have to put clothespins on our noses. The whole world would reek. That's why I'm not looking forward to growing up."

"There's a kid in my class who already stinks. He could use some of this." I finally find the razor and the shaving cream. "Here, you hold it." I untangle the cord and plug it in.

She holds the razor timidly. "What do I do with it?"

"Press the On switch when I'm ready. First we have to lather my hair."

We lather shaving cream on my head. Then I switch on the razor and start shaving my hair in long strips, from my forehead back. The electric razor vibrates in my hand. Izzy lets out a crazy giggle every time a clump of hair hits the sink. My head tingles against the razor and starts to feel cold in the bare spots, where the skin is pale. Shaving is harder than I imagined. I keep missing spots and I have to go back over them, and even so my head looks like a field of wheat where the tractor driver was dizzy.

Then Izzy runs the razor across the back of my head. She has a steady hand, and I feel the hair falling and falling, ghost breaths brushing the back of my neck while my old life as a regular boy falls away.

I look totally different. Like the captain on *Star Trek*. My eyes grow bigger and wiser. I'm a whole new person. A holy person.

"Do you hear my mom calling?" Izzy says.

"No! Just finish. Hurry!"

CHAPTER 19

I forgot.

How could I forget class pictures?

They're on Monday. It's Friday, and I'm bald. Izzy couldn't have known. She never has to sit through class pictures.

When Ma first came in and saw me, she screamed, although Izzy and I had flushed most of the hair down the toilet and used the thick plush towels to mop up the water. Ma wanted to know how we could trespass in her private bathroom, how we could make such a mess, and didn't we know we could have hurt ourselves? And whatever possessed me to shave all my beautiful black hair?

Dad came in and looked around, blinking. I could practically hear the numbers grinding in his head while he tried to add it all up. Son + razor + crazy neighbor girl = no hair. Ms. Mumu was right behind them.

"How could you do this, Anu?" Ma shouted.

"There's nothing wrong with being bald!" I shot back. "Bapu was bald!"

Ma gulped. "So this is about Bapu?" she asked in a quiet voice. "You wanted to be bald like him."

I couldn't answer. My eyes burned. Izzy stood there mesmerized.

"Don't you know razors are sharp and dangerous?" Dad said.

"You use your razor every day!" I shouted, not sounding very holy.

"That's different. I'm a grown-up," Dad said, and kneeled in front of me the way Bapu did. The hurt welled up in my chest again. Dad looked at me the way Bapu used to, with his eyebrows pulled together. "Tell me what's going on," he said, but I couldn't speak.

Now Ma, Dad, Ms. Mumu, Izzy and I are sitting in our good living room, where only guests sit on the stiff couches with cushions that don't bend beneath our butts. Ms. Mumu and Izzy sit across from the three of us, as if we're facing off at a duel.

I, for one, am meditating, floating above the scene. I give up all worldly concerns—the stunned look on Dad's face, Ma's tight jaw. I know she's thinking of hiding every sharp object—scissors, knives, the pink lady razors she uses on her legs. Dad's probably wondering exactly how many hairs I flushed down the toilet. Two to the power of ten.

Ms. Mumu's mouth plays at the edge of a frown. "I thought the kids were in the backyard. Izzy has a treehouse out there. I went outside and found them gone. They know they're not allowed in this house. But I suspected they'd come back here."

"Children must be monitored at all times," Ma says.

I close my eyes. I'm a holy boy—I have empathy. I feel the fear in her voice. She thought I would cut myself. She thinks I'm going crazy. She turns to me. "Do you want to tell us why you did this, sweetie?"

"My head was hot."

"We could've taken you for a haircut." She's not convinced.

"I don't think they've done any harm," Ms. Mumu says. "They were experimenting. Why, when Izzy was five, she cut off her bangs."

I raise my brows at Izzy. She cut off her bangs? She's even cooler than I thought. Her bangs grew back and now they form a straight line across her forehead.

"Maybe you shouldn't have left the scissors lying around," Ma says.

"Hasn't Anu ever done anything naughty while you weren't looking?" Ms. Mumu asks.

I drew pictures on my bedroom wall when I was three, but Ma doesn't mention that. She and Dad had to repaint my room.

"My hair will grow back," I say.

"But that's not the point, is it?" Ma says.

"You'll look fuzzy, like a Chia Pet," Izzy says, and giggles. Ms. Mumu nudges her.

"Your pictures are Monday," Ma says. "What will I send to your relatives? To Auntie Biku?"

"Send them a bald picture," I say.

"Anu!" Ma glares at Ms. Mumu. "How could you have allowed this to happen?"

"My word!" Ms. Mumu presses a hand to her heaving chest.

"Priti, it wasn't Martha's fault," Dad cuts in. "She can't watch them every second, and she did go looking for them. We all trusted them to follow our rules."

Ma throws him an angry look and then brushes imaginary dust from her pants. "We should at least know where they are—"

"Kids will be kids," Dad says. "Wouldn't you rather they shave their heads than stare at the computer all day?"

Izzy and I trade glances. We did spend a while on the Internet. We found www.shave-your-head.com, but it was for older people and punk rockers, not holy boys.

"At least he didn't shave his eyebrows," Izzy says.

Ms. Mumu chuckles. "He looks quite good bald, don't you think? What about Captain Picard on *Star Trek*? Or Michael Jordan?"

"You do realize he's got to go to school like that?" Ma says. "The kids will make fun of him."

I think of Curtis and the other kids. I don't care what they say.

"Look, if you'd rather find another place for Anu to stay after school, I understand," Ms. Mumu says.

Dad shakes his head. "We know it wasn't your fault. We just wanted you to be aware. Anu misses his grandfather. The two were quite close."

How does Dad know anything about Bapu and me?

"Of course," Ms. Mumu says.

"The thing is, not knowing why he's done it," Ma says. "And why Izzy helped him. Worrisome, really."

"I think Izzy understands Anu, just a little," Ms. Mumu says. "She was very young when she lost her father, but she misses having him around. Perhaps together, she and Anu wanted to pay tribute to lost loved ones." Ms. Mumu gives me a caring look that makes me melt into the floor. No, not pay tribute. I'm the only one who can bring Bapu home.

Izzy's gazing into her lap. Maybe she's trying not to cry. I bite my lip.

Ma softens a little, and stands up. "I'm so sorry. Well, this was all just a bit of a shock. . . ."

"We appreciate your willingness to watch Anu after school," Dad says. As they walk to the door, I wish the grown-ups would all shut up so I could get on with becoming a sadhu.

After the Mumus leave, Ma lets out a long sigh and collapses into an armchair. "What do we do about you, Anu?"

I didn't realize there was anything to be done.

"Give him a wig," Dad says, and sits on the couch with his hands behind his head.

Ma lights up. "Not a bad idea, Rijoy."

"I was joking," Dad says. "He looks fine hairless."

"What about the relatives?" Ma says. "I have a hundred people on my list to receive photos. I ordered extras. How will I explain?"

"There's nothing to explain!" I cover my head with my hands. "And I'm not wearing a wig!" How will I become holy with fake hair? I'll look like Andy with the omelet on his head.

My skull feels smooth. A newborn head. Nothing but skin and bone separates my enlightened brain from the world now.

CHAPTER
20

Ma Googles for the closest wig shop: www.wilsons-wigs-for-all-reasons.com. For once, I wish my computer was broken.

"Just over on Chico Road," she says.

"I'm not going. My hair will grow back. Then I'll let it grow out longer and longer and get tangled like the holy—"

I cover my mouth.

"Holy what?" Ma gives me a piercing look.

"Holy smokes. Holy Toledo. Holy cow."

I pull on a woolen hat, which scratches my bald head, and the three of us climb into the car.

Wilson's Wigs for All Reasons is at the end of a strip mall. Inside, it's like the Halloween shop. Blond wigs, long wigs, curly wigs, red wigs, brown wigs, even white wigs on Styrofoam heads. There's a bald boy with his mother on the other side of the store. He looks like an egg, a familiar egg. Andy! He waves at me and I wave back, then shove my hands in my pockets.

The man behind the counter, with a nametag reading BERNIE, is obviously wearing one of the brown wigs, which has slipped sideways on his head. He smiles and nods. "I'll be right with you folks."

Ma and Dad and I sit. Ma pulls off my hat, grabs a black shaggy wig and puts it on my head. I look like Elvis Presley. Dad and I laugh.

In the mirror I catch a better glimpse of Andy.

"He's gonna come out of this just fine," Bernie says to Andy's mom.

"The doctors say he's doing well. Right?" Andy's mother runs her hand over his head.

Andy nods, but it seems to take all his effort.

"That's the best we could ask for." Bernie hands Andy's mother a box and says as they leave, "I sure do wish you folks the best."

I have an urge to run after Andy, to shake his hand and tell him everything will be okay, only I don't know if that's true.

Ma and Dad glance at each other. I take off the fuzzy wig and try on another one, a black one with fine, straight hair.

"I look like a girl," I say, taking off the wig.

"How can I help you folks?" Bernie comes over and glances at my head.

"We need a wig until his hair grows back," Ma says.

Bernie measures my head all different ways. The tape measure feels cold against my skin. "I have just the right hair system for you, young man. Synthetic fibers. Less expensive than human hair, and the color won't fade."

"What about real hair?" Ma asks.

I don't want to wear someone else's hair!

Bernie drapes the tape measure around his neck. "We can custom-make one, ma'am. Takes a few weeks."

"We have two days!" Ma's voice rises.

"Ma, I can go like this. Or not have my picture taken!"

Dad stands. "It's okay. We don't need a wig."

"Wait—" Bernie says. "I have his size in Hair-for-Kids. You'll love it. Machine-made cap. Durable!" He disappears and comes back with a black wig. It's perfect. It could almost be my own hair.

Ma and Dad appraise me. How will I become holy this way?

"This will do," Ma says.

"Just let him go bald," Dad says.

"All our friends will think—" Ma hesitates. "He is not going bald. We're doing it."

Bernie rings up the wig, puts it in a box. My lungs tighten and twist. I'll give the wig as an offering to Shiva.

CHAPTER
21

I'm out in the backyard with Izzy. Unger couldn't come over. He's too busy counting cash from selling baseball cards.

Ma monitors us through the kitchen window. She probably thinks Izzy is a bad influence.

I'm practicing rolling. It's not as easy as it looks, doing somersault after somersault. I could roll on my side, but all the famous holy men do somersaults. Izzy brings a stopwatch, recommended on www.become-a-holy-roller.com. People around the world try to copy Ludkan Baba. He's a fast holy roller, clocked in at fifteen miles per hour. See, Bapu? I can become like the holy men.

But my speed still sucks, and my head hurts. I need a helmet.

"You have to use your arms," Izzy says. "Like this." She pushes off with her hands and does three perfect somersaults. She's a better holy roller than I am.

I copy her, but I'm still slow.

Izzy walks ahead of me, picking up sticks and clearing the way. Lawn cuttings stick to my pants, my shirt and my woolen hat. My clothes are wet and stained, but I keep rolling from one side of the yard to the other.

"Not bad," Izzy says.

"Is my time any better?"

"A bit, but rolling here isn't the same as rolling to school. You'll need help, and I can't go with you."

I stand and brush the dirt and grass from my jeans. I hadn't thought of that. "Tell your mom you want to see what a real school is like."

Izzy screws up her nose, where the freckles gather in a clump. "My home *is* a real school. Ma says I learn a lot more at home than I would in an institutional setting."

"Don't you want to make friends?"

"I have friends, the other homeschooled kids. We meet twice a week, Tuesdays and Fridays."

"Don't you want to know about recess?"

But her mom says no, so I go inside to call Unger.

I carry the cordless phone into my room.

"You have to *what*?" Unger's voice gets all high when he's surprised. I can hear the crash and beep of the video game he's playing.

"Come on, Unger. I need your help." I explain to him about the sadhu. The same sadhu who has spoken to ghosts, brought back dead loved ones and healed even the sickest people. I expect

Unger to say no, to tell me he won't pick up garbage off the street, but instead he says, "Cool! Are you going to perform miracles?"

I hold the phone away from my ear. Unger's right. I have to do something miraculous. But what?

After Ma and Dad go to sleep, I'm lying backward on the bed, my feet on the pillow. The holy men turn upside down and backward, so why can't I? Then I get up and stand in my pajamas in a sliver of moonlight and hold my right arm straight up in the air. Sadhus always hold up their right arms, which makes life way more difficult. They can only use the "dirty" left hand, the hand used to wipe their butts. I wonder about left-handed people—how do they feel knowing their left hand is considered dirty?

I wonder if my sticking-up arm will shrivel like the sadhu arms in the Guinness Book of World Records. The sadhus never cut their fingernails. The nails keep growing and growing, like Pinocchio's nose, and then they curl under.

I keep an eye on the window for a glimpse of Bapu. The fingers of my right hand tingle and my eyelids droop. What does a sadhu do about gravity pulling the blood downward? Now my whole hand tingles. Now my arm. And my muscles are tired. I should have lifted weights. Then I would have been able to keep my arm in the air longer. I crumple to my knees, and just as I think I see Bapu's outline shimmering against the window, I fall asleep.

I wake up on the carpet in a patch of sunlight.

My arm hurts. I must have held it up for an hour last night. I run to the bathroom to look in the mirror for a sign of holiness. The carpet made a pattern of dents on the side of my face, and a hint of fuzz grows on my head. I'm an inch closer to holy today. I feel the sacred power trickling into me.

Ma and Dad bustle around, pouring themselves milk and cereal and gathering their papers for work. Ma puts the wig on my head and adjusts it. "Maybe he should wear the bicycle helmet to keep it on," she says to Dad.

"I'm not wearing any helmet!" I shout.

"We could get him a hard hat, for now," Dad says.

"Well, wigs don't usually fall off. This should do," Ma says. "Promise you'll wear it for the pictures."

What about what I want?

"Promise," she says.

"I promise."

She says she'll call the principal to explain my situation.

Ma and Dad are in such a rush, they don't notice that I don't eat my cereal. Sadhus meditate in caves for twelve years and fast for days, accepting only offerings, water and cigarettes. Since I don't smoke, I'll have to settle for offerings and water.

After Ma and Dad leave, I take off the wig and put on my hat. It's a cold day anyway. Nobody will notice. I stuff the wig in my backpack.

Unger meets me at the bottom of the driveway. It takes quite a while to roll down over the gravel. I didn't factor in my backpack, which gets in the way. My lunch will be squished, especially the banana, but who cares, since I'm fasting? I nearly roll over Unger's boots.

"Are you training for the Olympics, or what?" he asks.

"I'm copying Ludkan Baba. Can you carry my backpack?" I unstrap it and hand it to him. He puts his pack over his left shoulder, mine over his right. Unger is pretty strong.

"I wish I could see Lucky Baba," he says, walking in front of me as I roll. Good thing we left early. This is going to take forever. I stick to the grass by the side of the road.

"Ludkan Baba," I say. "You'd have to go to India."

"Do you have to roll all the way? We might be late. Like, we won't get there until recess."

At the end of the block, I realize he's right. I might have to cheat. But for now, I stick to the plan.

A fat kid and a skinny kid, like Laurel and Hardy, fall into step beside us. The fat kid is Roland; the skinny kid, Matt. "What's he doing?" Roland asks. "Is he, like, weird or something?"

"He's becoming a holy man to perform great wonders," Unger says.

"Whoa—how do you do that?" skinny Matt says. "Will I be a wonder boy if I roll too?"

"He's retarded," Roland says.

"I am not retarded," I shout. "I'm studying to be a sadhu."

"What's a sadhu?" Roland digs in his nose. He's wearing a Big Dog T-shirt that pulls tight around his middle.

"You know, those amazing men who can stick hooks in their backs and hang from them? They can stop their heartbeats and hypnotize cobras. They walk across hot coals and their feet don't even burn." I don't know why I'm saying these things. The sadhu in cousin Prem's video was just a boy sitting on a mat.

A crowd of kids tags along behind us now. Unger walks proudly ahead of me, kicking rocks out of the way as I roll. My arms are getting tired, but I'm getting better. Soon I'll have a direct holy phone line to Bapu.

95

"So, can you turn my peanut butter and jelly sandwiches into egg sandwiches?" Matt asks hopefully.

"I don't do magic," I say, rolling. "But I stopped traffic by sticking up my hand and making a force field. But it only works sometimes."

"Like *X-Men*?" Matt hops along, sucking on a lollipop.

"I'm my very own X-man." I'm so full of it. "But mostly I tell fortunes." Where did that come from?

"Like reading crystal balls?" Matt's eyes go wide.

I think of what Izzy told me about the amazing Stella, who spits out fortunes at the Mystery Museum. "For a quarter, I'll write your fortune on a piece of cardboard." What am I saying? To be holy, I have to perform great wonders.

"That's pretty cheap," Roland says. "I have a whole roll of quarters."

"Only one prophecy per kid," I say. "Per day."

For the next five blocks, I gather followers like a rolling stone gathering moss. I'm getting better at rolling, and another kid rolls behind me. Everyone cheers us on to see which of us can roll faster. I win. But when we get near the school, we both stand up and brush off our clothes. I've rolled enough for now. My stomach grumbles and my head feels light, but I am much closer to being holy.

CHAPTER 22

We have class pictures first thing. My teacher, Ms. Lumpenberger, stares at my wig. It looks so close to my real hair, you wouldn't notice it if you didn't know I was bald underneath. The principal must have told her.

Word is getting around about my rolling. The kids whisper and pass notes.

"Class pictures in five minutes," Ms. Lumpenberger says in her clipped voice, as if she cuts out her words with scissors. "Let's comb our hair and straighten our clothes." She stares right at my head, which is neat and tidy already. If I try to use a comb, the wig might fall off.

She comes up to me, kneels next to my desk and lowers her voice. "How are you feeling, Anu?"

"Just great." Does she think the wig will interfere with my

97

brain or something? I smile at her, a holy smile. My body vibrates from head to toe. I have a few dents and bruises, all part of becoming a sadhu.

She hands back my "Home and Family" essay with a big "A+" on the front. "Imaginative," she wrote.

I'm happy about the essay, but I hate class pictures. Lining up reminds me of lining up to get shots. A yucky sludge sits in the bottom of my stomach, below the fluttering butterflies.

Then I notice Andy standing a few kids behind me in line. What possessed his mother to choose fluffy blond hair? Everybody knows he doesn't really have any hair. The wig looks like an egg experiment gone horribly wrong.

Nobody's talking to him. Kids glance at him, but they don't make fun of him. Curtis is too busy fixing his hair at the end of the line. The kids move forward, one at a time. Ms. Lumpenberger stands near the front, helping kids adjust their clothes. She wipes snot from a few noses.

Unger's behind me, and we make faces at each other. He's standing with another friend, Tyler, talking about the latest episode of *The Simpsons*.

The photographer runs back and forth, from tripod to kid, adjusting a chin, adjusting the light, turning knees sideways as if we're puppets.

I keep glancing back at Andy. He looks miserable.

My wig itches. The weight suffocates my holiness. I became bald on purpose, and my mom made me cover it. I wish I could show Andy the sadhus of India. I wish he could have seen the vision of my Bapu the way I saw him, feel the gods passing through me and into the bugs and the water dripping from the leaves.

When it's my turn, Ms. Lumpenberger smiles. "You know, the hair looks fine," she says, then leans down to whisper, "Your parents could teach Andy's mom about choosing the right wig!"

That's when I know what I have to do. I promised Ma, but some things are more important. Just as the photographer is setting up for my shot, and Ms. Lumpenberger walks back to help a girl adjust her barrette, I pull off the wig. Everyone gasps. I don't know what my head looks like. I don't care. Cool air rushes over my skin. Bapu, my dear Bapu, this is for you.

I throw the wig onto the floor and step forward to have my picture taken. A couple of kids giggle, but others stare, and I know Andy is staring too.

"Hey, kid, creative haircut!" the photographer says, and laughs. He's chewing gum and smells as if yesterday's cigarettes accidentally exploded in his pocket. "You sure you want to do this?"

"I'm sure," I say. "Haven't you seen Michael Jordan or Captain Jean-Luc Picard from *Star Trek*?"

"Yeah!" Unger says behind me, and punches his fist in the air. So do I, and a few other kids punch too.

Ms. Lumpenberger grabs the wig and runs to me as if I'm on fire and the wig is a hose.

"I don't want it." I step up onto the platform beneath the warm spotlights.

The photographer looks at me and cocks his head to the side. "We can do something with this." He adjusts the lights, and Ms. Lumpenberger stands there holding the wig toward me. What's the big deal about hair, anyway? We're all people underneath.

It's over in a few seconds and I walk away. When Andy goes up to have his picture taken, he pulls his wig off. He looks toward me and grins. I grin back and punch the air, and something sacred passes between us as he steps up onto the platform.

CHAPTER

23

Famous bald celebrities from www.bald-to-the-bone.com:

Homer Simpson
Captain Jean-Luc Picard from Star Trek
action star Vin Diesel
Moby, the musician
Samuel L. Jackson
Yoda
Kermit the Frog
Pablo Picasso

Another bald person from history: Mohandas K. Gandhi, aka Mahatma Gandhi, the peaceful brown man who led India to independence in 1947. The country broke free from the British, and here

I am today. If it weren't for Gandhi, I would probably be stuck in a boys' boarding school in India, where I'd have to eat slop and wear a scratchy uniform and get my knuckles hit if I whispered in class.

I fold the note, then stuff it in the slot in Andy's locker as I pass.

I can't really say I'm like those famous bald people. First, I'm not famous (yet), and my hair is already growing back. I'm destined to grow sadhu dreadlocks to show my true worship of Shiva.

After school, I roll home, but I'm much slower, since I've accepted only offerings today—which amounted to half a peanut butter sandwich and a piece of apple. By now, Bapu should be much closer. I should have a direct channel to him in the spirit world, but he's fallen quiet. I ignore the queasy feeling this gives me—Bapu might be sleeping. Do the spirits sleep halfway from here to the ozone layer? Why doesn't Bapu come back? I have to be patient.

I gave my lunch away to about five different people. A few followers straggle along, and Unger becomes my assistant. He takes orders for fortunes and drops the quarters in a plastic Bartel's drugstore bag.

"You should charge a dollar a fortune," he says. "Then we'd be rich."

"I don't want to be rich." I roll to the edge of the schoolyard. "I have to give up all material things to become holy and open a line to my grandfather."

"Does that mean you're giving away your computer?" Unger's eyes light up.

I shake my head. "No way—I need the Internet."

"Drat." He kicks an empty Coke can out of the way. "We need to start picking up the garbage, and the cans for recycling."

A few girls come up with coins jingling in their pockets.

"I don't want any bad omens," a girl named Sylvie says. All her features squish together as if pinched by a clothespin.

"Your fortune is your fortune." Unger takes the coins and scribbles on his notepad. "Bad or good, you take what you get."

"What a rip-off." She drops another quarter in the bag. "If the first fortune is bad, I want another one."

Unger writes the second girl's name on his notepad. "I'm guessing you want only a good fortune too?"

She sticks out her chin. "Whatever my fortune is, is what it is." She throws me a defiant look and marches off with her friends.

"Listen to the quarters," Unger says, shaking the bag. "You have to do about five hundred fortunes."

"There aren't even five hundred kids in the school," I say.

"Okay, twenty-seven, and not all from our grade. You hooked some little kids."

Unger keeps taking off his glasses to wipe them on his shirt, the way his father does. Unger's getting pretty good at being a salesman, but I don't know how I'm going to get good at writing fortunes before tomorrow.

By the time we reach Izzy's house, I'm so hungry, my stomach is turning inside out. Bapu's voice comes back to me. *You must remember to have supper.* I wonder if he knew I would become a sadhu. I stand up and wipe the dust and bits of grass off my clothes.

"Do we have to go inside?" Unger asks on the doorstep.

"Izzy's cool. You'll see."

The door swings open, and the scent of potpourri drifts out. "Ah, you've brought a new friend!" Ms. Mumu lets us in. She's breathless, as usual. Unger stares at her as if she's Godzilla.

"His name is Unger. He's my accountant." I lead him to the kitchen. We have to suffer through homework first, but I figure it's part of my sadhu training. Unger looks all around and pets the cats and chomps on the cookies. Izzy plays with her bead necklaces and stares at him.

A Holstein cat jumps onto the table and sniffs my head, then rubs against me and purrs.

"You must've rolled over catnip," Unger says. The cat jumps to the floor.

"Rolled?" Ms. Mumu asks, sitting heavily on the chair across from us.

"We were playing a game at school." I glare at Unger. Ms. Mumu looks as if she just ate a sour grape, but says nothing.

Unger's quiet after that. I gobble three of the oversized cookies before I even notice, and Ms. Mumu says, "You didn't eat today? Didn't your mom send you to school with lunch?"

I stop, a huge lump of cookie stuffed in my cheeks. "I did a lot of rolling and got hungry," I say, a few crumbs falling on the plate. She looks worried. I've been made. It's not so easy becoming holy.

Unger and I glance at each other, and Izzy stares at both of us.

Ms. Mumu's brows furrow. "Look, at least eat something healthy."

She makes egg salad sandwiches, and I can't refuse to eat or she'll tell my parents, who will hold a family conference and who knows what else. So I eat. I'll return to my fasting tomorrow. One can't become holy overnight.

In Izzy's room, she and Unger help me cut out squares of cardboard from her mom's old manila file folders. Unger keeps saying "Whoa, cool" and touching the curiosities. Izzy is being so patient. Unger picks up the shrunken head and dangles it by its hair. "Is this real?"

Izzy frowns at me, as if to say, *Why did you bring me this dork?* "Of course it's not real, silly. It's made of rubber. The real heads are at the Mystery Museum."

"I want to go there," Unger says.

"You have to take two expensive buses and the ferry," Izzy reminds us.

"We'll have enough money soon." Unger keeps sticking the fake plastic snot up his nose. "This is really cool."

"Could you wash it when you're done, please?" Izzy says in an irritated, grown-up voice. "And I expect a cut of your earnings."

Unger puts the snot down. "No way. We got the fortunes."

"But I'm working for you. I don't work for free."

"Ten percent," Unger says.

"Slave wages," replies Izzy. "Thirty."

"Twenty."

"Twenty-five."

"Deal," says Unger. "Anu and I split the rest."

"I don't take money," I remind him. "I'm becoming holy."

"Cool—seventy-five percent for me," he says.

"Greedy," Izzy says.

"Whoa, wait. Have you forgotten what this is all about?" I say. "This isn't about telling fortunes. It's about my grandfather. I have to bring him back."

Izzy waves the blank sheets of cardboard. "But you have to be holy, don't you?"

"Yes, but—"

"Then do good things for people. Make them happy. How many pieces do we need?" She snips away with a pair of pink scissors. I wonder if those are the same scissors she used to cut off her bangs.

"I have twenty-seven orders for fortunes." I unfold the paper I scribbled on all day.

Unger snatches the paper from me. "Even Rolly-Roland asked for a fortune? Tell him he'll die from being too fat."

"That's mean," I say, and a new thought occurs to me.

I can help kids like Rolly-Roland. I can make him happy, if only for a minute. I write:

~~Rolly~~ Roland: You will exercise and eat many fewer Twinkies. In about tenth grade, you will lose weight and go out for football. Nobody will call you Rolly anymore.

"Are you sure you should be that specific?" Izzy asks. "Stella says good fortune will come our way. That's all. She doesn't say, *'You will receive one million, five hundred and fifty dollars and ten cents on your seventeenth birthday—'*"

"But he has to make the fortune worth a quarter." Unger pushes the glasses up on his nose. "So he has to be sort of specific."

"Are fortune cookies specific?" Izzy says. "No, they just say, *'You will have good luck,'* or *'Things are looking up.'*"

"I'm not a fortune cookie," I say.

"You agreed to do this," Unger says. "You're the one becoming a holy man, not me."

"Wait, wait. No fighting." Izzy puts her hands in the air, palms forward.

Unger takes off his glasses and cleans them vigorously on his shirt, then puts them back on.

I scratch out Rolly-Roland's first fortune and write:

> Lakshmi, the goddess of abundance, will bring you health and good fortune. Look for signs of new life sprouting in the garden.

Unger frowns. "I think Roland is Presbyterian, and he doesn't have a garden, just a weedy lawn."

"Minor points. All lawns are gardens," Izzy says.

"You've been to Rolly's house?" My mouth drops open.

Unger's ears turn red. "We played baseball there once."

"It doesn't matter. The fortune's good." Izzy tosses the shrunken head in the air and catches it. "Anyway, Roland can still be Presbyterian and get his fortune told, can't he? And weeds are new life sprouting from the garden. Let's move on."

Unger shakes his head and checks Roland off the list.

For Matthew, who always gets bad grades, I write:

> Ganesh, the elephant-headed remover of
> obstacles, will clear the way to your success. But
> only if you study hard and find a tutor.

"Too specific," Izzy says.

Unger takes off his glasses and cleans them again. Unlike
Clark Kent, who looks exactly like Superman all the time,
Unger looks like a whole different person with his glasses off.

"Telling him to find a tutor isn't specific," he says. "Horror-
scopes in the newspaper always say specific things, like 'Stay
home and eat a TV dinner tonight. If you go out, the evening
will be a flop.'"

"Horoscope, not horrorscope," Izzy says.

"You read the horoscopes?" I stare at Unger.

"They're right next to the comics." His face grows redder.
"Hard to miss."

"Whatever." Izzy shrugs and shakes the shrunken head at
me. "Fine, be specific."

I choose somewhere between specific and useless. I'm performing good deeds, small feats of wonder to make others' lives
better. I'm on the fast track to holiness.

For Shari, a girl who doesn't want to go to the dentist:

> Pray to Lakshmi and ask for an abundance of
> strong teeth. Brush after every meal, and stop
> eating chocolate bars for lunch.

CHAPTER
24

I've been surfing the Internet to learn more about how to bring back Bapu. I'm opening a channel to the Cosmic Consciousness, to Brahman, pure fuzzy existence. Sadhus know that the normal human mind can't grasp the Cosmic Consciousness. Only mystic holy men know the Cosmic. They strive toward the inner light. They break away from earthly bonds and enter the spirit world. Before the ninth or tenth century AD, the holy men sometimes sat on dead bodies, or sacrificed humans. They ate flesh and blood. The thought gives me the creeps.

These days, I read, most sadhus are peaceful. They meditate, read scriptures, recite mantras and perform acts of self-sacrifice to open channels to the spirits.

I must follow their example and leave behind my normal human mind, find where Bapu floats, waiting for me before he disappears forever. But the universe is huge, ten million to the power of ten billion miles deep, Dad might say. Part of me races up, out to catch Bapu, while part of me starts to drift back down to Earth, and I don't know why.

After all, I'm performing great acts of kindness, sharing my lunch with Andy, Unger and Tyler. If they hand me pieces of sandwich or a couple of bites of banana, I accept. "I can only take offerings and water," I say.

The kids love my fortunes. I meditate at the Shiva shrine in the woods (sometimes with Izzy there, singing and playing with her beads), and I hold my arm up in the air every night.

But it's hard to stay holy with kids like Curtis around. I bet that even the fastest sadhus sometimes fall off the track. When Curtis knocks me over and calls me bald bin Laden, I trip him and he hits his mouth on the ground.

The recess monitor stomps over to yell at both of us. We get detention. I've never tripped Curtis before. I am sick and tired of being called names, but I'm not being very holy.

And I should have remembered the fall rains in the Pacific Northwest. I get soaked rolling to school, and one day I roll right over dog poop.

I jump to my feet. "It's all over your back!" Roland says. "Ew!"

"Unger, you weren't paying attention!" I try not to hurl at the smell.

"I *was* looking!" Unger shouts, the rain running down his face. "It's hard to see everything, you know. The poop blended in!"

"Was it wearing camouflage gear?" I shout.

"Why is it always up to me?" Unger shouts.

110

"I saw it." Skinny Matt points. "I saw the poop before you rolled over it."

"Then why didn't you say anything?" I run to a yard and lie on my back, rubbing my jacket in the grass.

Matt shrugs. Roland is laughing so hard, after all I've done to give him hope in a cruel world.

Unger's shaking his head. "There's poop on your pants too. On the back."

I stand up and try not to cry. Wouldn't do to have a kid my age blubbering at school. But we're so far from home, I can't turn back now. I'm stuck between poop and school, and I don't know what to do. Bapu, this is all for you.

"I have to go home," I say.

"You'll get in trouble," Unger says. "Go to the nurse."

"Does she keep extra jeans?"

"She might," Matt says. "When I got a paper cut, she helped me a lot. They almost had to airlift me to Harbor hospital—"

"For a paper cut?" Unger pushes the glasses up on his nose. They're fogged over and covered with droplets, and the rain makes his nose slippery.

"The cut was deep," Matt says.

I don't know what scares me more—getting in trouble for going home, or going to the nurse for help.

I'm already here. The nurse.

Right near the school, the rain turns to hail and the kids all run inside. I hope the hail blasted the poop off my clothes.

Under the overhang near the main doors, I take off the jacket. The back is still stained and stinks. I try to see around to the back of my soaked jeans. I can't see but I can smell it. I rush inside to the nurse.

111

A few kids screw up their noses as I go by. "Who farted?" some-one asks. "Did you cut the cheese?" Word will get around fast.

"Anu Ganguli, what brings you here?" Nurse Edmonds asks. She's square, like a Rubik's Cube. Her office smells like a hos-pital, and I think of Bapu in his hospital bed. I think of Ma at work. I hate hospitals with the doctors in white coats and the smells of alcohol and sickness. Hospitals swallow mothers and grandfathers and don't give them back. Nurse Edmonds ushers me inside. She says nothing, even though I know she smells the poop on my clothes.

She closes the door behind me. "How can I help you, Anu?" She remembers my name, maybe from vaccination days.

"I rolled over dog poop."

"Rolled? Let's see what we can do for you." She rummages in the drawer and comes out with a big plastic bag. "Here, put your jacket inside." I can tell she's breathing through her mouth.

I drop the jacket.

She ties the top of the bag and takes it into the bathroom, then comes out and closes the door. "I think your jacket is his-tory, but we can try to use bleach. The material is breathable and washable, but the color might fade."

"You'll wash it here? You have a washing machine?"

She nods. "But you'll have to stay inside until it's done."

"Thanks." I'm so grateful.

"Did you get any on any other part of you? In your hair? Oh—" She sees I don't have much hair.

"Just on my jeans." I'm standing there, dripping water and who knows what else on the floor.

"Take them off too and I'll wash them."

I'm not taking off even poopy jeans in front of a square Rubik's Cube nurse. "I need an extra pair."

"I don't have any." Her brows furrow. I can see the cubes moving in her mind. "Maybe we can call your mother—"

"No, don't call my ma. She doesn't know—"

"Doesn't know what?" She looks at me as if she already knows the answer.

"That I was rolling."

"Is it against the law to roll?" She glances at my Chia Pet head.

"I guess it's not."

"Word is out about your business venture with Unger. He's quite the young entrepreneur."

I swallow, wondering if she plans to tell my parents.

"Do you have any other clothes at school? Gym clothes, maybe?" she asks.

Gym clothes! "I have shorts. I don't want to wear shorts around school."

She goes to the phone. "Then I'll call your mother. I have a work number for her. She can bring you jeans."

"No, she can't. You don't understand. My mom is a doctor. She can't ever leave work."

Nurse Edmonds gives me a funny look. "Ever? You mean she sleeps there? Perhaps she can leave work when her son has a problem."

"I don't have a problem. I don't need my mom."

An image flashes before me—Ma striding through the halls, waving a pair of jeans, confronting me about the poop and how dirty it is and how a grown-up needs to watch me at all times.

"Well, okay." Nurse Edmonds's brows furrow. "Then what—"

"I'll wear my shorts." I take my locker key out of my backpack.

She takes the key. "I'll get them for you."

I have to thank the gods for small blessings.

But I still have to walk around school in my gym clothes with goose bumps rising on my skin. Curtis opens his mouth to call me a name, but says nothing. Maybe he knows I might trip him again. He's losing steam.

By recess, my pants are dry. Thank the gods. And the nurse. I get my math textbooks from my locker and hang out in Ms. Lumpenberger's classroom.

Sylvie comes in, her features pulling into the center of her face. "You know the fortune you gave me, that good things would come my way if I only wait? And that my lucky numbers are three and fifty-seven?" She slides into the seat beside me.

"Yeah?" That was the most general prophecy I've made so far. I chose three because she's one of three kids in her family, and her parents have three poodles. I chose fifty-seven because it's the number on her house.

"It didn't work. My dad played the numbers in a bunch of scratch-off tickets last night, and he lost."

"I'm sorry, Sylvie. The fortunes, they're just a game."

She sticks out her bottom lip. "My mom didn't get a raise at work."

"I didn't say she would—"

"You said good things would come our way."

"They still will, I'm sure, you know." I'm tripping over my words. "I mean, good and bad. Good and bad things happen to everyone."

114

"I don't want any more fortunes. Tell Unger I want my quarter back." She strides out, brushing past Andy.

He comes in and slides into the seat beside me. He bites his lip as if he wants to ask me something. I want to ask him questions too, like whether he's afraid he's going to die like Bapu died, but I just stare at the pages in my old textbook.

Close up, I can see the thin blue veins under the skin of his jaw. He hasn't worn his wig since class pictures.

"Thanks for what you did, Anu." He glances at the fuzz on my head. He touches his own head, still smooth and hairless.

"I didn't do anything."

He waves the piece of paper I put in his locker, the list of bald people. "Thanks for this too. I showed it to my mom. I didn't tell her that I had my picture taken bald. I don't know what she's going to say when the prints come back."

"I don't know what my mom will say either, but it doesn't matter. Bald is cool."

"Bald is cool." Andy and I slap our hands together.

"Could you do my future?" he asks. "You know—a prophecy." His eyes shine, and he leans toward me and holds out a quarter.

I don't take the quarter. I keep staring at him and blinking. I can't tell Andy's future. I don't know his future. His future is life or death. He has to know that.

"I can't." I lean back, and the desk squeaks.

"Why not? You gave everybody else one, like fortune cookies!" He grins with excitement.

"Only the gods know our futures. They know everything, and I'm not a god." Someone else is talking, a boy who knows that hidden forces make the world turn, that gravity holds us to the ground, that I can't change any of that.

115

"What about the fortunes?" Andy asks. "My friend Nina wants one—"

"I'm not doing prophecies anymore. They were for fun, not for real. Unger wanted to make money. Now he's rich and he can invest those quarters in a retirement account."

Andy's face falls, and he tucks the quarter back in his pocket. "I think you need a thousand dollars to open a retirement account. That's four thousand quarters."

"Then Unger will have to start a new business."

"You think I'm going to die, don't you?" Andy's eyes are calm, matter-of-fact.

My throat tightens. "Andy—I don't think you're going to die, okay?" I lean over and do something I've never done. Usually I would think it was yucky. I put my hand over Andy's. His fingers are so warm, they're on fire. I wonder if he has a fever. "You–are–not–going–to–die."

"I know."

I take my hand away. "You know?"

"Yeah—my mom took me to the Mystery Museum, and Karnak told me. He waved his wand, and then a few weeks later, my tumor started to shrink."

"You got to see him?" Izzy told me about Karnak.

"You have to drive way out to Port West and take the ferry all the way to Divine Island. Karnak is awesome."

"What does he look like? What does he do?"

"He's a cool magician. He does all kinds of tricks. He says he comes from the planet Karnakian, where everyone has special powers."

"No kidding—did you have to pay to see him?"

"My mom paid." Andy's face sobers. "You have to walk through a scary part of the museum to the theater in the back. I kept my eyes shut the whole time and my mom led me."

"How could you keep your eyes shut?" I'm leaning toward him, nearly falling out of my seat.

"I opened them for a second and this huge shrunken head bounced around and almost bit me."

"It was actually moving?"

He nods and nods. "And there were two mummies—they were actually alive."

"Alive? What do you mean, alive? Izzy didn't tell me that."

He leans in close and lowers his voice. "They move. I saw. One moved its arm and the other one moved its mouth. Totally freaked me out."

"Moving mummies? Did anyone else see?"

"I don't know—I didn't tell. I squeezed my eyes shut and my mom led me back to see Karnak. He does two shows per day, only on weekends. He's awesome."

"Whoa—and your tumor shrank? Did you ask him to take it away?"

"I asked him to make me well." Andy sits back in his seat. "The other kids were asking for silly things. Like, they wanted him to pull a rabbit out of a hat or make the silk scarf change color from green to red. Oh, and he pulled a quarter from behind one kid's ear."

"And what did he say when you asked him to . . . make you well?"

Andy sticks out his lower lip and glances out the window. "He said he could do anything, anything at all, and that he

117

would grant my wish, of course, because he's Karnak, and Karnak has great power. He gave me a magic statue of himself. I keep it by the bed."

"That's amazing." I sit back, hit in the brain by a meteorite. "Congratulations, Andy."

"Yeah, thanks." He gets up and slings his backpack over his shoulder. "But I wasn't asking you about that, anyway. I just wanted to know what my mom would say about the class pictures."

He walks toward the door, light on his feet. Karnak the Magician must be like one of the gods.

The bell rings. I gather up my books as Unger comes in wiping his glasses on his American flag T-shirt. "I've been looking all over for you. I heard Nurse Edmonds made you wear your gym clothes. You poor kid." He sits beside me and jingles the bag of coins. "Three more! But you're on your own today."

"I'm not doing prophecies anymore. Give back the quarters."

"But—"

"I can't really see the future, and you know it."

"So what? Stella tells fortunes at the Mystery Museum, and she can't really see the future either."

"How do you know about Stella?"

"Izzy told me."

I narrow my gaze. "When did she tell you?"

"I called her last night. I'm going over to talk business today. We might have new customers, maybe the homeschooled kids."

"Did she tell you about Karnak the Magician?"

"Yeah, why?"

I stand up and head out to math class as the students rush in, damp and yelling after recess. "You're going to Izzy's? I thought you said homeschooled kids were weird."

"Yeah, but Izzy's cool. So, what do you say? Should I charge the homeschooled kids extra?"

"No new prophecies. That's it. I'm finished."

"Aw, Anu!" He stands in the hall while I keep going. Unger and Izzy are getting together without me? Why didn't they invite me?

CHAPTER

25

Kandarpa, the ancient Hindu Cupid, has leaf-green skin and rides a parrot the size of a horse. Like the Western Cupid, Kandarpa carries a bow and arrow. The shaft of his bow is made of sugarcane, and his five flower-tipped arrows are the five human senses. He flies around shooting arrows and dropping pulsing hearts into people's eyes so they fall gaga in love with each other, which is probably what happened to Unger and Izzy.

I can't believe Unger's going over to her house. Why do I even care? Who wants to hang around with a funny-faced, skinny girl who wears beads and collects curiosities?

Because Izzy's cool, that's why.

It doesn't matter. I can't go to her house today. After she gave me my clothes back, Nurse Edmonds told me she'd called my ma, and now I'm waiting at school for her to pick me up. I can practically see her anger puffing down the road. She had to leave work early, something that has never happened in the history of the universe.

Her Subaru pulls up into the guest parking lot, and I grab my backpack and race out through the rain to the car. My heart pounds.

She keeps the engine running as I slide into the passenger seat and fasten the seat belt. The shoulder strap tightens across my neck. Ma's car has crumpled Kleenex tissues lying around, a pack of gum on the dashboard and a traveler's mug of coffee in the cup holder. Ma's wearing her white coat and tapping the steering wheel. Her fingernails have been bitten to the quick. I brace myself, but Ma touches my head. "Are you okay, Anu? Had quite a day, didn't you?"

"Yeah, I'm fine." I look at her face, watch for a trace of annoyance. Ma just looks tired. Dark rings smudge the skin beneath her eyes.

She pulls out of the parking lot and drives home. I relax in the warmth of the car and watch my rolling route out the window. The yards and houses and grassy slopes look smaller from here. It takes so long to roll, and only a minute to race by in a car.

"Do you want to tell me what's been going on, sweetie? I spoke to the principal and Nurse Edmonds."

"I'm sorry to make you leave work, Ma."

"It's okay. I had a short day anyway."

My jaw drops open. A short day? Ma?

I stare at her profile. She comes from a whole other family, a family of straight noses and soft chins. Not hooked noses and jutting chins like Dad and Bapu.

"What did Nurse Edmonds tell you?" I ask.

"Everyone seems to know about you and Unger hatching another moneymaking scheme."

"I didn't keep any of the money."

"But you're rolling to school." She glances at me as she turns the corner. We're almost home.

"To be closer to Bapu."

"By rolling? I don't understand."

I can't tell her. I'll sound crazy. "Just stupid, I guess."

"Bapu's gone, Anu."

"Do you have to remind me? He's not gone! You and Dad *want* him to be gone. Getting rid of his Shiva statue. Cremating him and throwing his ashes in the river. Giving Auntie Biku his things to take back to India. What if he wants them here?"

"I know you miss him. We still have some of Bapu's things. Perhaps when you grow up, you can take them with you."

"You didn't . . . give them all to Auntie?"

Ma shakes her head. "They were lying all over the house, and seeing them was very painful for Dad."

"What about me? What about what I want?"

Ma touches my cheek. "I wish I could make it easier. But . . . no more rolling, okay? And Ms. Mumu says you're not eating your lunch."

I don't answer.

"I hear you're trying to become a holy man—"

"Sadhu," I blurt.

Ma's fingers tighten on the steering wheel. "Sadhu. You have to take care of yourself, baby. You're growing. You have to eat. You'll become very sick if you don't eat."

"The sadhus grow too, and they don't get sick—"

"You can make the decision about becoming a sadhu much later, when you're a grown-up."

"I'm moving closer to the gods."

Ma turns up our driveway, the gravel crackling beneath the tires. She presses the remote to open the garage door and parks inside, in the cold dimness.

"You don't have to move closer to the gods, sweetie. You can just be a boy. Be Anu, yourself. That's who Bapu wanted you to be. He loved *you*, Anu."

"I am being myself. My new self."

"Why did you need a new self?"

I play with the ashtray, opening and closing it. "I don't know. I want to be holy like the boy-Baba."

"Your old self was just fine. You don't need to be a boy-Baba. It's very important for you to be just a *boy*."

She doesn't understand. When I was just a boy, being myself, I couldn't run home fast enough through the woods to save Bapu. Holy men can do anything. They can fly, heal the sick, bring back the dead.

I'm sorry I didn't pray regularly, Bapu. I can't hold my arm up in the air for years—I fall asleep. I can't fast—I keep getting hungry. I'm not a good holy roller either. I thought I was helping people by telling them good things about themselves, but I don't know everything about every person. I didn't know that Andy was getting better. I didn't know that Karnak had all the power.

Look where I am. Sitting in Ma's car wearing once-poopy clothes.

123

CHAPTER

26

I dream of the Mystery Museum. The lights dim as I step inside. Shrunken heads line the shelves, their sewn-shut eyes following me. The heads grow to the size of huge party balloons bouncing along, whispering to each other. Probably trying to figure out where their bodies went.

I shiver from a phantom breeze and keep walking deeper into the museum. I try to ignore the skeletons dancing in the corners, wrinkled mummies sliding through the shadows. Fear clogs my throat, but I keep moving. A light glows in the back of the store. I step over headstones and swerve to avoid zombie arms pushing up through the graves.

A man steps into the light. At first, he's just a shadow, but when he steps forward, he comes into focus. He's tall and wears a shiny red turban with a glittering diamond in front. His third eye, the magic eye. He's hairy like Mr. Singh in the airport. He pulls his handlebar mustache and motions me closer. His tunic and trousers shine gold, and his shoes curl up in the front, like boats.

"You've come for your Bapu," he says in a booming voice that seems to come from my blood.

My heartbeat pounds in my ears. "Can you really bring him back?" Every moment rushes through my memory. Bapu spilling *dhal* on the stove, the smoke setting off the alarm. Bapu letting a bold chickadee land on his palm, taking me for long walks and teaching me about the gods. The glint in his eye when we hid from Ma and Dad. The time we drove to the beach by ourselves.

"Of course I can bring him back." Karnak winks. "I'm a magician. I can do anything." He waves his wand, and then I wake up. How could I have woken up just before the magic moment? Darn, darn, darn. Bapu could have come back. I would have woken to find him here, in solid form, able to touch me and read to me and hold a spatula.

It's just before dawn, and the first birds twitter in the shrubs outside. Bapu says everything happens for a reason. I dreamed about Karnak for a reason. Now I know what I have to do. I pick up the phone to call Izzy.

CHAPTER 27

"I'm not allowed to go to the Mystery Museum on my own," Unger says.

"Me either," Izzy says.

"But we have to go," I say.

We're in Izzy's room sitting cross-legged on the floor, in a circle, with two tiny rubber shrunken heads in the middle. I'm not sure why Izzy put them there—maybe to keep an eye on us. She's practicing Midnight Smoke, a new curiosity. A puff of smoke rises when she snaps her fingers. She's getting really good at it.

Izzy sighs. "I wish Karnak would help me pass the state test next month—"

"Then you have to go," Unger says. "Me, I'm asking for a million dollars."

"A million isn't that much anymore," Izzy says.

"It's enough for me. Start-up costs for my home business."

I don't want to ask what Unger has in mind for his next venture.

"I don't have enough money saved for the ferry," Izzy says.

"We have cash from Anu's fortunes," Unger says. "And I'll loan you the rest. I've been saving my allowance for the past three years."

"Thanks, Unger—I have a little allowance too." I unfold the bus schedule. "We leave Saturday. We'll take the seven o'clock bus from here." I point to the bus stop four blocks from my house. "We have to switch buses at Port North, and in Port West we can catch the ferry." I take out the map and unfold it on the floor. I trace the highway route to the ferry.

"Wow—that's a long way." Unger takes off his glasses and cleans them, squinting at the map.

"I've been way farther than that," Izzy says.

"By yourself?" Unger asks.

"Not exactly—"

"See?"

"Okay, enough," I say. "We'll leave notes for our parents, so they don't worry and call the police. Nobody else can know. Are we agreed?"

"Agreed," they say in unison, but Izzy casts a suspicious glance at Unger. "I think we should seal it with a blood pact."

Unger sits on his hands. "No way am I pricking my finger."

My fingers tingle too. "We don't need to seal it, Izzy. We trust each other, don't we?" I glance around, hoping she doesn't find some weird curiosity to bleed us with.

"Okay, then hands together," she says, and Unger and I let

out a sigh of relief. We put our hands together, one on top of the other.

"In case of a change in plans—cell phones?" Unger waves his phone, and I take mine from my pocket.

"I don't have a cell phone," Izzy says, looking disappointed.

"I'm sure everything will go fine." I put the cell phone in my pocket. I can't tell my friends about the worry growing inside me. Karnak is my last hope.

CHAPTER

28

I wake up at six, on schedule, but Ma and Dad are already up. I can hear them moving around and talking in the kitchen. What's going on? I flip open the cell phone and call Unger. He sounds wide awake. "My parents are up," I say. "We have to abort. But we can't wait too long. Tomorrow?"

Unger breathes hard into the phone, making a loud static sound. "Tomorrow, tomorrow . . . okay. Is there a bus?"

I'm unfolding the schedule again. "Yes, but it doesn't come as often. Can you call Izzy?"

"I'll take care of it."

We hang up just as Dad opens my door. "Rise and shine," he says. "I have a surprise for you."

He's dressed in clothes I've never seen—a plaid shirt, khaki pants and a cap. "Have breakfast and get your binoculars. We're going bird-watching."

Bird-watching? Dad?

And Ma made eggs that don't run! They sit in a fluffy pile in the center of my plate. There's freshly squeezed orange juice, toast and mango.

"How would you like to go to the Nisquat Reserve?" Dad asks. "Lots of birds there, I hear."

The day is clear, no rain in the forecast. A tingle of anticipation runs through me. I'm not supposed to be thrilled about bird-watching with Dad. Not after the disastrous outing with Auntie Biku. Dad can't tell the difference between a robin and a Steller's jay, but he's finishing his food and he's got a book with him, *Birds of the Northwest.* He's shoving it into a huge backpack, and Ma made us lunch.

I run to my room—float, really—and take my bird-watching gear from the closet. I bring my binoculars, and my poncho, just in case.

"Have fun, okay?" Ma touches my stubbly head before Dad and I leave.

I get to sit in the front seat.

The car windows are like a fishbowl all around me as Dad drives south along the highway. We listen to the Rolling Stones, his favorite band, and sing along to "You Can't Always Get What You Want." When we arrive at Nisquat, he parks in a huge lot and we stop at the visitor center for a map before heading off on the trail.

Everyone here is into birds. Some people carry big, expensive binoculars. Dad and I set off down a long trail—over five miles all the way around—and right away, we see a gaggle of Canadian geese.

"Look, there!" Dad points and lifts his binoculars. "Ducks in the pond."

I'm skipping and hopping along. "I never came here with Bapu."

"He didn't know about this place," Dad says.

"I wish he could've known." I spot a hawk overhead, wings spread. "Maybe he could've seen an owl."

"I think the owls are hiding—too many people on the trail." Dad stops at a clearing and points the binoculars west, toward the sea. "Look, there, it's a bald eagle."

A crowd gathers as we all train our binoculars on a huge eagle with a white head and black feathers.

"The white head means he's over five years old," Dad says.

"How do you know?" We keep walking.

"I've been reading the bird book."

I glance at him sidelong. Was Dad reading the bird book just for me? "Dad, do you believe in ghosts?"

He looks at me and laughs. "Where did that come from?"

I shrug. "Could someone who died come back? Maybe once or twice, in a dream? And then start to fade away?"

Dad frowns. "I expect that maybe if someone came back, he might be afraid that someone else couldn't let him go. A loved one, perhaps."

"But what if he wants to come back and be with us?" I say before I realize what I'm saying.

"How do you know the ghost is a he?"

"Just . . . hypothetically." I copy one of Dad's big words.

131

"Hypothetically . . . anything is possible."

I blink at Dad, not sure if he's the dad I know, the dad stuck in numbers. Then he says, "What I mean is, in the new quantum physics, scientists now know that our minds play a huge role in what we see. The smallest units of matter have both wave and particle properties. When you're looking at them, they become real. They acquire particle properties. When you're not looking at them, they're waves of possibility and probability, in more than one place at a time."

"You mean a ghost can be everywhere, like a big wave, and when I see him, he's a real ghost?"

"Are we talking about Bapu here?"

"Maybe."

He's silent. We stand at the edge of a marsh and watch the ducks weave through the reeds.

"Bapu's been hanging around you?" Dad asks.

"Sometimes." My voice is barely a whisper. "But not lately."

Dad takes my hand. "Come this way." We walk along a narrow bridge across the marsh. There's a bench in the middle, above the water. We sit there, and it feels as though we're floating in the pond with the birds.

"You know, maybe Bapu only stays because you want him to stay," Dad says. His voice cracks.

"How can he want to leave me?"

Dad puts his arm around my shoulders. "He didn't want to leave, Anu. But he did. I still can't believe it myself. I miss him every day, every moment. I'm sorry—"

"Sorry for what?"

"I'm sorry I haven't been such a great father to you." Dad

throws a pebble into the pond. The water ripples out in bigger and bigger circles and then goes calm again.

"You've been a good father, Dad." A big lump comes into my throat, but I'm not going to cry. I grip Dad's hand, way too tight. I don't want to ever let go. He doesn't know what I keep seeing: I'm back in the woods, and Bapu falls in the dirt, and I'm running and running and I don't know the way home. I didn't bring the phone. The branches hit me in the face—I'm too slow, and Bapu is slipping away.

I have to talk to Karnak.

CHAPTER 29

Dear Ma and Dad,
   Don't worry about me. I'm in good hands. Izzy, Unger and I are on a field trip. We'll be back tonight. We have to talk to Karnak. We need his help. I have to get Bapu back, and only Karnak can help us now. See you later.
Love,
Anu

I prop the note on Ma's purse on the kitchen counter, where I know she will see it. Dad snores in their room, but Ma could come out any minute. I'm wearing my poncho, since the weather can change in a heartbeat, and I stuff a couple of bananas in the pockets. I creep out the front door, closing it softly.

The cool morning nips at my face as I run down the driveway. I'm the last one to the bus stop. Dawn paints a strip of bright pink across the sky.

"What took you so long?" Unger says. "The bus will be here in, like, a minute." He's wearing a poofy parka and counting dollar bills.

"Hey, Anu," Izzy says. I've never seen her dressed for a journey. She's wearing purple tights, beaded boots and a long blue raincoat.

The bus chugs around the corner, belching stinky exhaust, and grinds to a stop. The doors fold away from each other like cards. Izzy marches right up the rubber steps. I follow, Unger last with the money.

I hold the railing, my heart pounding. We bump into each other as the bus leaves the curb and lurches down the road.

"Morning, kids!" the bus driver says. "Where you off to?" He's a young man, heavy, with a stubbly chin, and he must have accidentally poured a whole bottle of aftershave on his face.

"Port West," Izzy says.

"Great day for a ride, huh? No parents with you this beautiful Sunday morning?"

"We're on a field trip," Unger says.

"I'm babysitting the boys," Izzy says, standing to her full height.

"Oh yeah?" I feel the driver watching us in the mirror as we head toward the back, holding on to the seats as we go. The word *kids* brands us. Izzy gives me a wide-eyed look, and we sit near the window, the three of us hunched together. "That was close," she says.

"Babysitting?" Unger frowns, takes off his glasses and wipes

135

them on his jacket, which makes them even more smudged. "We don't need babysitting."

"Would you rather get sent home?" Izzy snaps.

"No fighting, remember?" I unzip my jacket and clean Unger's glasses on my shirt. "Why don't you get contacts?"

"My parents say I'm not old enough," Unger says. "Do you think the driver will tell the police?"

I shake my head, although I'm not so sure. "I think he believed her."

"Izzy doesn't look old enough to babysit," Unger says.

Izzy straightens her shoulders. "I look twelve at least."

Unger frowns. "What if he calls our parents?"

"He doesn't know who we are," I whisper.

An elderly lady gives us the evil eye, then faces forward again. We slide down in the seats.

Izzy presses her nose to the window. She absorbs the scene outside, hills and trees and houses whizzing by, as if she's visiting from another planet.

We're silent most of the way. The bus makes many stops and gradually fills with people; the sun moves higher and the day grows warmer. We change buses in Port North.

"Look, you can see the ocean!" Izzy presses her finger to the window. The sea glints through the trees to our right, to the north. The terrain opens into rolling pasture dotted with barns, horses and cows. To the west are the jagged Olympic Mountains. Wisps of white clouds cling to the peaks. I wonder if Bapu can float to the highest mountain. Then I think of the god Shiva, meditating on Mount Kailasa in the Himalayas, which are twice as high as the Olympic Mountains.

"Wow, cool!" Unger says. He stuffs the plastic snot up his nose. I can't believe he brought it with him.

We're so absorbed in the scene that we don't notice the bus turning into town and heading down toward the dock.

"Ferry stop!" the driver calls, and this is where we all get out. The wind whips in from the sea. We're at the very edge of the world, on a waterfront road lined with faded stores, a fish and chips restaurant, a clothing shop and a small run-down book depot. Ahead of us is the ferry building with a sign directing cars to line up to the right. We go inside. A bunch of sleepy people sit on long benches. Izzy grabs a ferry schedule. "The next one to Divine leaves in half an hour." She stands on tip-toe at the counter and buys our tickets.

I've never been on a boat so big. You could fit our whole school in here. The passenger area, lined with chairs, is as big as our gymnasium.

We slide into a booth near the window. Unger buys French fries, and we munch and stare out at the seagulls flying along-side the ferry, the mountain range turning hazy blue in the distance behind us. I'm seized by fear. We don't have our parents anywhere close.

"What if we get stuck there?" I ask. Izzy turns to look at me.

"I was just thinking the same thing." She glances toward Unger, who's off playing a video game. "We'll be okay."

My rib cage squeezes, but I force myself to breathe evenly. "I brought the phone." I take it from my pocket, the one Dad left for me to use in case of emergency. If I'd had the cell phone when Bapu died—when Bapu fell . . . The phone is on, a picture of a jester in the display window.

Izzy's lost in thought, her freckles gathering at her nose again. "I'm worried about my mom."

"Me too." Unger takes off his glasses and cleans them. "I told my mom where we were going, but she won't see the note until she takes a shower around noon."

We sit in silence until the driver cuts the engine and the ferry drifts into the bay. We watch out the window, all of us tense, but eager to see Divine.

"Whoa—it's a jungle. Look at all the trees." Unger goes out on the deck and we follow, the wind whipping off the sea. I feel a little sick.

"No, look, a few buildings!" Izzy says, pointing.

When the ferry docks and we walk off, we're in a forest. Thick fir, madrone and cedar trees grow nearly down to the water. Most people drive off the ferry. A few stragglers follow us on foot. Inside the ferry building, we go to the information desk to ask for directions to the museum. "Three blocks," the clerk says. "You can walk into town."

Relief. Old-fashioned, tall brick buildings mark the downtown strip—Divine Grocery, a small store. Art galleries, eateries, clothing shops—tourist traps, as Ma would say. We find the Mystery Museum in a tall, wooden A-frame, the name written across the top. I can't believe it—we're really here.

Through the dark, tinted windows, I catch glimpses of touristy things—key chains, postcards, sweatshirts, flag decals. People mill around looking at the framed pictures, the polished, petrified wood. We step inside and the floor creaks under our shoes.

"Whoa, this is sweet!" Unger pushes the glasses up on his nose.

"This is nothing like my dream," I whisper to Izzy. The museum buzzes with activity, kids of all ages, grown-ups from all over the world.

"You dreamed about the Mystery Museum?" she asks. "What did you dream?"

"Karnak was awesome." My heart thumps at the thought of him somewhere in the back room, waiting to make anything happen.

Tourists browse the T-shirt racks, and women gather at a glass case full of flashy silver jewelry. There's a 1950s gas pump ahead of us, about six feet tall, in the shape of a cowboy. A man drops a penny in the slot. The pump grinds, then spits out a flattened penny. Unger's already moving into the crowd, checking out the funny magic tricks. I lose him in the sea of faces. There's so much stuff in here, but none of it is really weird. Then I notice what's hidden in the back and up on the walls. Wooden masks with black, empty eyes staring; shields and totem poles; old weathered mounted antlers; spears; blades. I shiver, and Izzy takes my arm and pulls me forward.

"Look!" Unger appears in the crowd, pulls on a plastic finger that makes a loud farting sound. All the kids are gathering there, pulling on the plastic fingers. "The soap!" He waves the soap that makes you dirtier the more you use it.

"Come on, that's kid stuff," Izzy says. "Let me show you something really cool." She leads us to a big wooden contraption with a handle. The sign reads, X-RATED VIDEO FROM 1920S.

Unger's eyes go wide. "Naked ladies?"

"You think everything X-rated is about naked." Izzy drops a quarter in the slot. She stands on the step, cranks the handle and peers down into a glass viewer.

139

Unger and I crowd up on the step and peer through the viewer. A woman sits in an old-fashioned clawfoot tub. You can only see her head and shoulders above the water as she washes and splashes, sticks a bare foot in the air.

"This is X-rated?" Unger says.

"Believe it or not, back then it was X-rated to see a woman's ankle." Izzy lifts her skirt to her knee. Her tights are really purple.

The woman gets out of the tub. She's wearing a towel. Then she walks out of the picture and it's over.

"That's it?" Unger says.

"That was pretty daring for the 1920s," Izzy says. "Come on, I'll show you Stella." She leads us to the left side of the store, but Unger keeps getting sidetracked, and we stop at a set of shelves with Divine Island coffee mugs imprinted with names in alphabetical order: Adam, Alan, Amy, Betsy, Bob, Chet, Dan, Elizabeth, Frank . . .

"No Izzy," Izzy says. "There's never an Izzy."

"Or an Unger," Unger says. "There's never even a 'U.' "

I know there won't be an Anu. I never bother to look. I never realized that Unger and Izzy wouldn't find their names either. I feel closer to them now, closer because we're here together, together in trouble, all of us with funny names, looking for holy.

Stella sits high inside a glass case with a purple velvet backdrop. She wears a red hat covered with glitter. The plastic mannequin stares at us through marble eyes set back inside her head, as if a real person hides inside the plastic shell.

"Whoa, Stella." Unger opens his mouth and his hot breath fogs up his glasses. He fumbles in his pocket for two quarters and drops them in the slot. We jump backward as Stella whirs to life. One arm rises while the other waves across her crystal ball. Her long, tapered fingers don't move, but her arms bend at the shoulder. Her lips are painted red. A creepy, clanking sound echoes out. There's a clicking, and a card drops out through the slot. Unger grabs it and reads, " 'You will find your calling and inherit a great fortune.' See, I told you!"

"It says 'inherit.' Not make crooked business deals," Izzy says. "My turn." She drops her quarter in the slot, and Stella comes to life again, her frozen plastic arm moving over the crystal ball. The fortune drops from the slot and Izzy reads, " 'Your future lies in the limelight. You love to perform.' "

"That's true." Unger points at her. "You like to dance with your shrunken heads."

"I do not!" She shoves Unger in a playful way and he shoves her back. The Indian Cupid is at it again. I roll my eyes. Izzy's fortune could be for anyone.

"Your turn, Anu," Izzy says, but I shake my head. I don't believe in Stella anymore. I want to believe in her, but she keeps the fortunes in a pile and they come out one by one, in order, as people put their quarters in the slot. I hate that I know that, and I hate that the Mystery Museum doesn't seem so much of a mystery. I want it to be; I want it to be a mystery with all my heart.

We're somber going to the door that opens into the dark room beyond.

A woman stands in the way. She looks like a prison guard in her gray uniform. A man and his son and daughter are waiting to get in, talking in excited voices. A big handwritten sign on the door reads:

See real mummies, shrunken heads!

Consult Karnak the Magician!

Not for the faint of heart.

Rated R for disturbing images.

Enter at your own risk.

All children under 18 must be
accompanied by parent.

The three of us stare at the last sentence as if it's written in Japanese.

CHAPTER 30

The blood stops flowing in my veins. The room dims with a sense of doom. This is too important. We can't turn back now. I think of Bapu about to fade away forever. I think of myself running through the woods, Bapu falling.

"Andy didn't tell me about the sign." I turn to confront Izzy. "Why didn't you tell us?"

"I didn't know—the sign wasn't there before!" she says.

"We're under eighteen," Unger whispers. "We'll never get in."

"We could sneak in," Izzy says. "Turn around and pretend to look at the postcards. Maybe the guard reads lips."

We all turn and stare at the postcards. "We could distract her," I say.

"She doesn't look distractible," Unger says. "She's planted by that door."

Izzy picks up a postcard of the Space Needle in Seattle. "We could slip inside with the other kids."

"That won't work," I say. "She'll see."

"We could pretend our parents are just around the corner," Izzy says. "I've done that before."

I glance over my shoulder at the woman, a stone statue by the door. "Somehow I think she won't buy it."

"Then we go home." Unger's got his glasses off and he's cleaning them vigorously on his T-shirt, over and over again.

"I'm not going home until I talk to Karnak," I say.

Unger props the glasses back on his nose and they promptly fog up again. "Look, Anu. Maybe an Indian holy man can fly, but nobody has ever brought a ghost back to life. Your grandfather is gone for good, okay?"

"Unger!" Izzy says in a warning voice, and I look at them and realize Unger and Izzy have been talking about me behind my back. They think I'm crazy.

"We have to try," I say. "We came this far."

Izzy puts her hands on her hips. "How exactly do you plan to get in?"

We watch the guard talking to a family. ". . . only let ten people in at a time," she's explaining.

"We'll just have to talk to her." I square my shoulders.

"I'm not talking to her," Izzy says.

"Me either." Unger shakes his head.

My feet are moving forward and I'm standing in front of the guard, who stares down at me from skyscraper height. My mouth moves, but nothing comes out.

"Can I help you, son?" A line of bright pink smears her cracked, thin mouth. I try not to stare at the lipstick gathering in the fissures of her lips. I point back toward Unger and Izzy. "My friends and I have to see Karnak," I say.

Her penciled eyebrows rise. The father and his kids are watching me. "Is that so? And why is that, young man?"

"We have important questions for him. We really need his help."

The woman's cracked mouth widens into a sort of smile. "You kids are too young. Did you see the sign?"

"We're mature for our age. We can handle the mummies."

"No kids allowed alone. We've had little kids pee their pants in there." She leans down toward me. Her breath smells faintly foul. "And your hair could turn white from fright."

The kids gasp with excitement. The father is looking at me. Why does this woman call me a young man if she thinks I'm just a little kid?

"My grandfather died." There, I said it. He *died*. "He always wanted to bring me here, but he never got a chance."

"Then why didn't you get your mom or dad to bring you, honey?" So now I'm no longer a young man. I'm a honey.

"We took two buses and the ferry and saved our money."

"Rules are rules," she says, straightening.

"Please, just this once?"

"Come back with your parents."

"But it's so far!"

We're somehow deflated when we step outside the Mystery Museum. The sun climbs high in the sky, shining too brightly and making us squint. All the happy people bustling by, some with big ice cream cones, seem distant, in another world.

We drag our feet down the street, along the blocks back to

the ferry. I think of Dad and me on the Nisquat trail and Dad telling me about quantum physics and how anything is possible. Izzy and Unger are talking about how they didn't really want to go into the Mystery Museum anyway.

I take the cell phone from my pocket. I wonder if Ma or Dad tried to call. They must have. They must be running around in a panic. Suddenly I hate that I left them a note instead of telling them in person. But they would never have let me go to the museum alone. But how can I be sure? I stare up at the sky and anything is possible. Then I flip open the cell phone, but the display is dark. The battery is dead.

I use the pay phone by the grocery store. Ma picks up after half a ring. My heart pounds through my throat. "Ma?"

"Anu!" she says with relief in her voice. "Are you all right? Where are you? We tried to call—"

"I'm on Divine Island."

"Are Izzy and Unger with you? Their parents are worried sick."

"I know. I'm sorry. We had to come—"

"Do you have any idea how worried we've been?" I can tell I'll be punished for a year.

"Can I talk to Dad? Can he come here? I need him to come here, Ma."

"Unger's parents told us where you were. Dad's already on his way. He's on the ferry by now. He's coming to get you. I decided to stay here in case you showed up at home. Your cell phone isn't working."

"I know." I let out a sigh of relief. "We'll wait by the ferry."

I hang up, and Izzy and Unger are staring at me with horror in their eyes. "We are in so much trouble." Izzy screws up her

146

nose. We wait in tense silence until Dad drives off the ferry in the Subaru. He pulls over and parks and we all pile inside, Izzy and Unger in the back, me in the front. Dad's face is calm. He doesn't look angry. "Put on your seat belts," he says, then snaps open his cell phone. "They're all here, and they're fine," he says to Ma. "I'll bring them back on the next ferry. Two hours."

Two hours? "Dad," I say. "I know I'm in trouble. Really big trouble. Thanks for coming. I can get in trouble later, but for right now, I need you to take us to the Mystery Museum. I need to talk to Karnak the Magician."

"Karnak the Magician, huh?" Dad's voice trembles oddly. "Is the museum in town?"

I point, and he starts the engine and pulls out into the thin stream of traffic. We're in town in two seconds. We're all quiet, wondering what will happen next as Dad parks in front of the grocery store. "I've never been to Divine," he says. "Quaint, isn't it?" He unlatches his seat belt and turns to us. His face is a little sad.

I'm not sure what to say. We get out of the car and walk along the main road, not talking. This is so weird.

We're standing outside the Mystery Museum again.

"You came here to see the magician." Dad looks down at me with the same quiet look.

I nod. Izzy and Unger gather around, and then Unger says, "We couldn't get in. We had to have a parent—"

"Unger." Izzy elbows him.

"Let's go in, shall we?" Dad says.

CHAPTER

31

In the dim back room, our footsteps creak on the wooden floor. The room is smaller than I expected, the ceiling lower. From high on the walls, masks with black, hollow eyes stare out at us. Dried white hair sticks out of the tops, as if the masks have gone crazy being alone up there all these years. Stuffed birds are frozen in flight, forever trapped. No place to fly, no windows. Two gigantic totem poles rise like ancient pillars ahead of us. Otherwise, all the curiosities hide in glass cases. I didn't expect glass. I expected the mummies and shrunken heads to dance out at me, brush my hair with their bony fingers.

"Whoa, cool." Unger rushes forward to a tall glass case. Inside, a shrunken man the color of mud stands on tiptoe, one hand across his chest, the other across his stomach. His shriveled skin shows the outlines of ribs, intestines, and organs underneath. He's bald, his eyes are shut, his lips pull back to reveal crooked white teeth. I let go of Dad's hand and race after Unger and Izzy.

"Desmond the Desert Mummy," Izzy reads on a plaque. Desmond's wearing a black cloth over his private parts.

"Whoa—sweet." Unger pushes the glasses up on his nose. "Look. He still has a mustache, eyelashes—and teeth."

I secretly thank the gods for not turning Bapu into a mummy. "And fingernails," Izzy says.

Dad hangs back, letting us explore.

"Look, another one!" Izzy shouts. We run to the next mummy. "Desdemona!" She's even more shrunken, with orangey-red hair, an open mouth as if she's screaming and empty eye sockets sewn shut. She's wearing a red loincloth and knee-high boots tied around her legs with white string. She gives me the creeps. A huge lonely feeling presses on me. Maybe I've become truly holy and I can feel the sadness of the world. The mummies' sorrow surrounds me.

"I don't like the mummies, Dad," I whisper. "I don't think they want to be on display."

"I know, Anu."

We pass cases full of real shrunken heads, bigger than Izzy's replica. Their skins are black. There's even a shrunken torso of a Jivaro Indian headhunter. I should drool and gasp like Izzy and Unger, but instead I want the gods to set the shrunken people free. They don't belong here, being stared at like this. Any one of them could have been Bapu.

Kids are filtering in with their parents, and the room comes alive with the hum of conversation. This doesn't seem like a mystery museum at all anymore.

149

We find Karnak's stage in the back corner. I sit between Dad and Izzy in the front row. There's nothing much on the platform, just a podium and a table with a black cloth. Soon the guard steps onstage and turns on the microphone. There's a high-pitched ringing sound before her voice comes through. "Welcome, boys and girls, ladies and gentlemen! Are you ready?"

"Yes!" the kids shout.

"Are you set?"

"Yes!" Even Izzy and Unger are shouting. I sit on my hands, but my foot won't stop tapping the floor.

"Prepare yourselves for the one, the only, the ancient magician who can make anything happen! Karnak!"

The audience roars. I try to sit still, but my heel keeps kicking the chair leg. I put my hands in my lap. Suddenly, I can hear every breath in the room, every movement, every sniff.

A man steps from behind the curtain. He's bald! He's carrying a black top hat and wearing a white shirt, black pants and a black cape tied at the neck. He carries a black wand. He's stooped, as if he's tired, the cape hanging like a bad Halloween costume from his shoulders. He's not wearing a golden jacket or a turban with a diamond. No third eye. He doesn't have a mustache or shiny shoes that curl up in the front. There's no halo around him.

You're not Karnak! I want to shout. The Karnak of my dreams can wave his wand and leave a trail of sparkling light. My Karnak commands attention. He's like a walking rainbow.

Karnak adjusts the microphone. "Good day, boys and girls," he says in a high, nasal voice. He clears his throat. "I apologize— I'm a little under the weather. Cold, sore throat, the works."

The kids shift in their seats.

He clears his throat again. "How many of you want to see me pull a rabbit from a hat?"

The kids let up a roar, and he puts the hat on the table, waves the wand over it, and produces a floppy-eared white rabbit. The kids clap. Most of them are young. I feel old. The guard rushes onstage and takes the rabbit.

Karnak performs other silly tricks, and the more he does, the sillier he seems. He's just a man with a runny nose, and I want to cry. How will I bring Bapu back? How?

When Karnak's done, he tells kids to come up to the microphone that is set up in the audience and ask him to do a trick. A little boy steps forward holding his mother's hand. "Can you give me a pony?" he asks. "For my farm?"

Karnak winks, waves his wand over the hat and produces a plastic horse. He comes to the edge of the stage, kneels and gives the kid the pony.

"That was a setup," Unger whispers, nudging me with his elbow.

I know this already.

Then Izzy and Unger drag me to my feet to line up.

"Can you make me pass the state exams?" Izzy asks eagerly at the microphone.

"You have to study hard, young lady," Karnak says. He hands her a plastic statue of himself. "Put this in front of you while you study, at least two hours a night. You'll pass."

"Wow!" She leaves the stage staring at the plastic doll.

Then Unger steps up. "Can you give me, um, a lot of money? A million dollars?"

Karnak shakes his head. "You have to work to earn your money, but if you put this in front of your mirror while you're

151

working"—he hands Unger a plastic doll of himself—"you'll have a better chance, young man."

The doll is exactly the same as the one he gave Izzy. I take my turn at the microphone.

"I want my grandfather to come back," I say.

"Where has your dear grandpa gone?" Karnak booms. He comes to the edge of the stage and bends toward me. That's when I see the caked-on, powdery makeup on his cheeks. He's just a person underneath. A person with a stuffy red nose.

I don't want to tell Karnak where Bapu has gone. A true magician would know the answer.

He straightens, and strides across the stage. "Okay, little man." He hands me the statue. "Here's hoping your grandpa comes trotting on home."

When we leave the Mystery Museum, my legs turn to stone and all the thoughts sink to the bottom of my brain. I don't care about anything anymore. Nothing at all.

CHAPTER

32

The ferry ride is a blur. I don't remember anything before we got home and I ran to my room and slammed the door. I don't feel Bapu in here. I don't feel him anywhere, and I don't know what to do. Ma's not home. She left a note saying she went clothes shopping. It's her way of unwinding when we're not around to bother her. I'm glad she's not here. I don't want to be close to anybody. I don't want anyone to come into my room, but Dad's knocking on my door.

"Go away!" I shout.

"Anu, we need to talk about Bapu."

"There's nothing to say."

"Yes, there is."

"Karnak was a fake. A total fake! He can't do anything! Just stupid tricks."

"Anu, I'm coming in." Dad opens the door. He sits beside me and puts his arms around me, and his spicy aftershave smell fills my nose. He feels solid and warm.

"All he did was give me that stupid statue. It's plastic! He gives everyone a statue. Why does he do that? How can he do that?"

"I know, I know." Dad's still got his arms around me and I lean my cheek against his chest. "I miss Bapu too. It wasn't your fault that he died."

My body goes stiff. "Ma told me."

"I know. But you still feel responsible, don't you?"

Tears sting my eyes.

"Bapu would've died no matter what." He lets out a long breath. "He had a massive stroke. It wouldn't have made any difference if the paramedics had arrived earlier. You did everything right. The result would've been the same. Do you understand, Anu? There was nothing you could've done. If you're keeping Bapu here because you want to be forgiven, you can let him go. Bapu doesn't need to forgive you. He knows it wasn't your fault."

A funny hiccupping sound comes from my throat. "How do you know he knows?" I whisper.

"Because I saw him too." I don't know if Dad's telling the truth. "But now he might need to leave and go to the gods."

I never thought of it that way. I never thought that Bapu might need to leave, that I might be keeping him here.

"I miss him so much," I say.

"So do I," Dad says. He is silent for a moment. "He read to me when I was a baby. He held me and took me bird-watching too."

"He did? When?" I pull away just a little, because I don't

want to be far from Dad. I don't want him to disappear the way Bapu did.

"In India, a long time ago. We did many things together. I'd forgotten. He was a help to me as a grown-up too. Aren't we lucky he came to live with us? We have to help each other now, Anu. We have to get through this together."

"But he doesn't even have a grave! I can't go and plant flowers."

"Yes, you can."

Dad takes me outside to Bapu's garden. "We can plant the winter vegetables. Look—some of the fall vegetables are still ripening."

A few small pumpkins hide beneath leafy vines. This is the first time I've noticed!

"We have to tend Bapu's garden now." Dad wipes his eyes. "Okay? It's up to us to remember him together."

CHAPTER
33

The Hindu god Ganesh is the Lord of New Beginnings. He granted a new beginning for Ma and me. She didn't get angry when she saw the school pictures of me bald. I don't know how the photographer did it, but he made me look handsome. I told her about Andy taking off his wig too, and she smiled.

Izzy got in trouble for going to the Mystery Museum, and now she's grounded for a month, which doesn't matter anyway since she's homeschooled. But I get to talk to her on the phone, and she's happy because she bought a bigger shrunken head at the Mystery Museum.

Unger got in trouble too. He has to help his dad figure out the taxes and do special housecleaning chores for two months.

I guess I got the best deal.

Dad and I hike through the woods again to search for barred owls. He wore his parka the first few times; then he bought a poncho like mine. I step into his giant footprints in the dirt. We follow the path far into the forest, until we can't see the mossy roof of our house. Dad's humming a Bengali tune. He keeps going around the bend and up the hill and finally stops in a clearing. We sit side by side on a log, and I'm so still, I could be a tree trunk. I barely breathe. In my days as a sadhu in training, I learned a few things.

Dad's leg is warm against mine, and the scent of his after-shave rises in the air.

"Soon, Shona, soon," he says.

I slip my hand in his. I like it that he uses my nickname. He's alive and warm. I'm tired of death, tired of trying so hard. The sigh of the damp wind, the rustle of fir needles, the faint disturbance of birds in the trees—it's all a part of this real, green world, where I can feel the raindrops cool on my skin, where I can hear Dad breathing and feel his heartbeat.

I'm sorry, Bapu, that I tried to keep you here in the rocks and the worms and the red bark of cedar trees, in the towering Douglas fir. Go to the gods, to the heavens. I can't go with you.

I'm beginning to understand the inner light, the light of being alive, new friends, seeing shrunken heads and a silly magician, bird-watching with Dad. This is my life, always moving with me and past me, shifting and changing color.

How long have we been sitting here? Through the mist, I see it now. The owl. It's been there all the time, pressing into the trunk of the giant Douglas fir. A feather flutters in the wet breeze, betraying the owl's presence. Then the rest of the bird,

157

its fluffy outline, comes into view, slowly growing clearer, as if a spirit hand just wiped a foggy window.

"There," I whisper to Dad.

"I see it too!" he whispers back.

We both hold our breaths, watching the mottled feathers fluffing as the owl readies for flight. Huge wings unfurl in silence, and the owl sails high through the trees and flies straight over our heads and away.

The rain comes down harder now. Dad snaps open a huge umbrella to cover us both, and I think of Bapu's story about the umbrella. The umbrella kept Jamadagni's arrows from wounding the sun. I can't help feeling protected under Dad's umbrella. Now I know what Bapu meant when he told me that story. I'm the sun injured by arrows. I was meant to sit under this umbrella with Dad, to keep the arrows from piercing my heart. And that's when I know, deep inside, that Bapu is gone. He will never come back. I turn to Dad and I start to cry. I can't stop. I've been immersed in a lake of sadness, and now invisible hands are lifting me out and wringing me dry.

CHAPTER

34

On a drizzly November afternoon, Izzy, Unger, Andy and I traipse back into the woods to pick up the Shiva statue. I can't leave him to drown in the winter rains. Izzy just graduated from being grounded—she keeps sniffing the air as if she's never been outside before.

Shiva still dances under the fir tree, but the soggy pillowcase is covered in leaves and pine needles.

"What's all that food around his feet?" Andy asks, pulling up his hood.

"Offerings," Izzy says. "Stale cookies and rice."

"I'm hungry." Unger wipes the mist from his glasses. "The cookies look good."

"Not for you!" Izzy sits cross-legged on the wet ground and

presses the palms of her hands together in prayer. "Thank you, Shiva, for helping me pass my exams."

Andy flops down beside her. "Thank you for helping my real hair grow back."

I kneel, Unger next to me. A warm fuzziness grows inside me. "And thank you for bringing together four best friends."

Andy grins at me.

Unger bows his head. "Thank you for making me help Dad clean the house. I found cash in my running shoe." He pulls a folded five-dollar bill from his pocket and places it at Shiva's feet.

Izzy snatches up the money and throws it back at Unger. "Gods are not materialistic!"

"I'll take the money," Andy offers.

"Okay, give it back, then," Unger says. "I have a new business plan anyway. We buy more shrunken heads and charge kids to come and see them."

"At whose house?" Izzy says. "I don't want a million kids in my room."

"They can't come to *my* house," Unger says. "My mom hates dirt. She'll make everyone take off their shoes at the door!"

While Izzy and Unger argue, Andy and I gather up the stale offerings. The rain has stopped and sunshine squeezes through the trees. If you hang around in the woods long enough, the sun will come out.

I tuck Shiva into my coat pocket. I bet he got lonely out here. It's time to tell Ma and Dad where he's been.

Later, when the sun's dipping in the sky, after we've had supper and Dad's working in his office and Ma's reading, I go to my room. Ma raised an eyebrow when I told her about Shiva, but she let me keep him. "Didn't he get cold out there all this time?" she asked, and her lip twitched as if she was trying not to smile.

Dad put on an extra-serious face. "You'd better warm him up." Now I keep Shiva on my bureau surrounded by offerings of fennel and rice.

I take Bapu's stamp album from my desk and leaf through the pages. The stamps are so strange and foreign, some old and yellowed, others touched with silver and gold. Lions, tigers, the map of India and rare flowers splash across the pages.

I bring the album to Dad's office.

His eyes water when he sees it. "Where did you get this?" he whispers, taking the album.

"Auntie Biku gave it to me."

"This—I had this when I was just a boy. Bapu gave it to me. I thought I'd lost it. But Auntie Biku had it."

"I thought it belonged to Bapu."

"It did. Then he gave it to me. You know, he kept extra stamps and things inside the cover." He lifts the cover and I see the stamps and other papers stuffed inside a pocket. "It's all yours now."

I take the album to my room. I pull the extra stamps from the hidden pocket. A thick piece of paper tumbles out—a faded photograph in black-and-white.

It's me.

I don't remember this picture. I don't remember wearing that weird white uniform, and my hair is shiny and straight and parted on the wrong side. But it's me. How did the picture get into Bapu's old stamp album? A shiver runs down my spine. I turn over the photograph. Written in a spidery hand on the back are the words *Siddhartha Ganguli, Darjeeling, January 1941.*

The blood pounds in my head, and my fingers shake holding the picture. My Bapu, at my age. He looked exactly like me. Why didn't anyone tell me? Auntie Biku! She held my face in her hands and cried, the tears pouring down her cheeks, and then she gave me this stamp album and told me something in Bengali. Was she telling me about the picture, and I didn't understand?

I touch my cheeks, feeling Bapu there, in the heat rushing beneath my skin. My throat goes tight, and I take the picture, run to the bathroom mirror. Could it be true? Could it really be? My eyebrows, my nose, my chin. My eyes. The same. The only differences are the hair and the uniform. I'm looking back to a time when I wasn't a glimmer in my father's eye, when my father wasn't a glimmer in Bapu's eye.

Bapu's smiling, the dimple in his cheek. He has one crooked tooth in front. Oh, Bapu, why didn't you tell me? Why didn't you say that I am you and you are me?

I dare to smile, hoping, wishing, wondering. It's there. How could it not be there? The dimple appears on my right cheek. Bapu's dimple. My Bapu's familiar smile.

AUTHOR'S NOTE

Although the Mystery Museum is not a real place, my inspiration came from the famous Ye Olde Curiosity Shop on Alaskan Way in Seattle, Washington, where you'll find most of the curiosities mentioned in this book, including a fortune teller, shrunken heads, the X-rated video from the 1920s, plastic snot, an old gas pump in the shape of a cowboy, the real desert mummies and many other novelties and collectibles.

However, there's no Karnak the Magician at Ye Olde Curiosity Shop. I made him up!

ACKNOWLEDGMENTS

My deepest thanks to my editor, Wendy Lamb; her assistant, Ruth Homberg; Erin Black; Marci Senders and all the amazing, hardworking people at Random House. As always, I'm grateful to my wonderful agent, Winifred Golden.

Heartfelt thanks to my critiquers: Kate Breslin, Lois Faye Dyer, Rose Marie Harris, Pj Jough-Haan, Richard Penner, Susan Plunkett, Sheila Rabe, Krysteen Seelen, Suzanne Selfors, Elsa Watson and Susan Wiggs.

Many thanks to astute readers who critiqued a later draft: Uma Krishnaswami, Marian Blue and Janine Donoho. Thanks to my cousin, Kamalini Mukerjee, for tidbits of advice, and my husband, Joseph, for listening to the whole book read aloud!

Love and appreciation to my parents, Denise Kiser and Sanjoy Banerjee, for their thoughtful comments.

I'm indebted to Leigh Holleschau of High Castle Books, for helping me with research and sending me *Stamps of India*.

Thanks to Ye Olde Curiosity Shop.

For Bapu's Bengali folktales, I consulted *Folktales from India: A Selection of Oral Tales from Twenty-two Languages*, selected and edited by A. K. Ramanujan (Pantheon Books, 1991). For information about sadhus, I referred to *Sadhus: India's Mystic Holy Men* by Dolf Hartsuiker (Inner Traditions International, 1993).

About the Author

Anjali Banerjee is the author of *Maya Running*, a novel for young adults, and *Imaginary Men*, a novel for adults. She was born in India, grew up in Canada and California, and received degrees from the University of California, Berkeley. At the age of seven, she wrote her first story, about an abandoned puppy she found on a beach in Bengal. She lives in the Pacific Northwest with her husband, three crazy cats, and a black rabbit named Friday. Learn more about Anjali on her Web site: www.anjalibanerjee.com.